Pining
FOR
LORD LOCKHART

JEN GEIGLE JOHNSON

LORDS FOR THE SISTERS OF SUSSEX SERIES

The Duke's Second Chance

The Earl's Winning Wager

Her Lady's Whims and Whimsies

Suitors for the Proper Miss

Pining for Lord Lockhart

The Foibles and Follies of Miss Grace

Follow Jen's Newsletter for a free book and to stay up to date on her releases. https://www.subscribepage.com/y8p6z9

FOLLOW JEN

Jen's other published books

The Nobleman's Daughter
Two lovers in disguise

Scarlet
The Pimpernel retold

A Lady's Maid
Can she love again?

His Lady in Hiding
Hiding out at his maid.

Spun of Gold
Rumpelstilskin Retold

Dating the Duke
Time Travel: Regency man in NYC

Charmed by His Lordship
The antics of a fake friendship

Tabitha's Folly
Four over-protective brothers

To read Damen's Secret
The Villain's Romance

Follow her Newsletter

CHAPTER 1

Sometimes, secretly, Miss Charity Standish wished she could be like everyone else.

She sat in front of a small mirror while her maid, Lily, pinned extra jewels in her hair, gifts from the Duchess of York, who waited downstairs for her so they could attend the first big ball of this season. Typically, Charity would have balked at such an extravagance and such an obvious attempt to shop her womanly wiles around the ton; but as she turned her red locks this way and that, she couldn't resist the pinpoints of light as they reflected off the candles. Was she vain after all? Certainly not. Appreciating the effect did not mean she valued her looks above all else.

After the Duchess of Sussex sponsored Lucy, and things went in a completely different direction for Charity's sister, and happily so, the Duchess of York determined to outdo her age-old rival, the Duchess of Sussex, and marry Charity off to someone truly renowned.

Charity humored the effort because it gave her another Season in London, access to anyone she would care to know, and the chance to build her reading salons and philanthropist activities. Come to find out, the Duchess of York was a secret bluestocking. She had been for years, since the days it was à la mode to do so.

She studied herself in the mirror, something she rarely took the time to do.

Lily sighed. "I wish you'd notice how stunning you are, miss." She laughed. "Everyone in the room is going to be watching just to have a look at you."

For the briefest moment, Charity let her maid's compliment have its way inside, boosting her vanity, but then she just laughed. "Perhaps I should wear a 'votes for women' sign as well then? Use the attention to garner some suffrage support?"

"Perhaps. That would certainly be something, wouldn't it?"

Charity studied her maid. "Do you think I should take all of this more seriously? Be about the business of getting married?"

Lily made a pretense of touching Charity's dress here and there before responding. "Now, it's not my place to say."

"When have I been a stickler for a person's place?"

"All the same, I remember my place. But here's what I think, plain and simple."

Charity smiled. Lily could rarely resist speaking what she thinks.

"I think there's a reason you're so beautiful, and it isn't just so that you can march around in your intellectual ways, telling all the men what they should think."

Charity's eyebrow rose ever higher on her brow.

"I told you it's not my place."

"And what is the reason for feminine beauty then? You

too are beautiful. And you are not parading about the ton trying to catch a husband."

"Those opportunities aren't mine." She laughed. "As if, the likes of me, parading about as you do." She shook her head. "I just think that you could keep doing all you do and be happily married while you do it." She curtseyed. "But that's all I'll say about that. You're ready and looking as beautiful as you ever have, if I do say so."

"Thank you, Lily. I couldn't do any of this without you. Nor would I try. If I do marry, it will be all because of your efforts, and that of Her Grace, of course."

The gown Charity wore sparkled to match her hair. The modiste had been instructed to outdo any other debutante that Season. And she had. Charity was certain of it.

Charity hadn't been looking forward to such a to-do about her clothing, but when she saw the gowns, she was admittedly pleased. They were beautiful in a manner she had not expected. They made her look strong and feminine at the same time. And she was infused with a new confidence.

She gathered her reticule and a fan to dangle at her wrist. She'd found the fan particularly useful if she wished to pretend not to see someone.

None of her sisters would be present at this ball, and none of her bluestocking friends. She was free to be and do whatever she wished if she liked, and a part of her wondered what it would be like to simply enjoy a ball. Must she always attend with a goal to spread important truths to the influential people in the room? Surely she'd done so enough; at this point, they all understood her standing on most things.

She tapped the fan into her hand. But there was that upcoming bill to consider. Logan, her sister Kate's husband, had sponsored it, and where they assumed it would pass without problem, a few of the Tories were up in arms.

She stopped her thoughts. Perhaps she would just simply attend the ball sponsored by one of the most influential women in London. If the bill came up, she would offer her opinion.

And Lord Lockhart might be there.

Her insides twisted up in excitable knots at the thought of that handsome and attentive friend. She couldn't stop the rise of color to her cheeks as she descended.

The Duchess of York stood at the base of the stairs as Charity descended, and the dear woman raised hands to her face. "I am enchanted. You, Charity, have far exceeded even *my* expectations." She turned to her husband who had just joined her. "Don't you think?"

He took a moment to glance her way. Then nodded. "Yes, she will be a credit to your name. Well done, my dear."

Charity dipped her head. "Thank you both. I don't know how to appropriately thank such a kind gesture."

"Think nothing of it. Do good with what we've given you. That's the best manner in which to thank my wife." The duke's oft-stern face showed off some of his laugh lines and Charity curtseyed to them both. "I shall do my best."

"That's a girl. And with a dress like that, and your natural beauty, I think the duke will be in high demand this evening, being asked for introductions."

He grunted as they exited the townhome. "True. You might wish to thank me again at the end of the evening. That or conquer the hearts of every man there in one go." He chuckled to himself. "You know, Her Grace was quite the catch. I had to fend off many a young hopeful in order to win her affection."

The two smiled in a rare moment of tenderness toward each other.

The duke helped them both up into the carriage and as Charity adjusted her skirts, she felt herself lucky indeed. Blessed. Thinking of Lily, she couldn't account for the different stations in people's lives, for their upbringing, for the incredible good fortune of some and the utter devastation of others. She only knew that where she had been given much, she must do the same in return.

They pulled in front of the Duke of Stratton's home. Thankfully, Lord Fellon held no ill feelings toward Lucy or the family for her sudden decision not to marry him. In fact, he may have been relieved. He was now courting a woman who made him laugh more than she'd even seen a smile appear on his face, and the two seemed well-suited indeed. If she were to guess, there might be an engagement announcement at the end of this ball.

She and the duchess entered on either arm of the duke, the doors opened wide to receive them. The house had been decorated with extra lighting. More candles than she'd seen anywhere lit the halls, the ceilings, the tables, everywhere she looked. And she could only be grateful at the extravagance. "Oh, I do like to actually see a person while dancing."

The duchess followed her gaze. "Oh yes, they've rather lit the place, haven't they?"

"Indeed." Her husband's attention was elsewhere, on a group of men exiting toward what Charity could only guess was the card room.

"And what if Charity needs to scare away a scoundrel?" The duchess tapped his arm with her fan.

"Our Miss Charity has proven herself capable of handling any sort of man, but if something untoward is at risk of befalling our guest, summon me immediately. They will rue the day." The spark of protective power that lit his eye gratified Charity. She nodded. "Thank you, Your Grace."

What would it have felt like to come to these sorts of events with her own father?

She could only guess. So far, she'd been well cared for by her brother-in-law, Lord Morley, and dear friends. But for a moment, that protective glint in the Duke of York's eye filled her with loneliness by comparison. She'd not experienced much of that protection in her life.

She stood taller, but perhaps the Duke was correct. She wasn't afraid to speak her mind if needed. For this, she'd learned to hold her own.

All this talk of catching herself a husband had softened her. She looked around, needing an unwitting victim of her tongue.

But the music began, and Lord Lockhart bowed to them all.

"Why, Lord Lockhart." The duchess almost clapped with glee, and Charity wished she could perhaps mellow her response to the old friend.

He behaved as the perfect gentleman with a side wink to Charity. "It is a pleasure to see Your Grace, as always. I look forward to our next salon."

She eyed her husband for a moment and then nodded. "I as well, that *musicale* was delightful." Her secretive smile made Charity laugh. She didn't know if the Duchess enjoyed their meetings more for the actual topics presented or for the intrigue of hiding her involvement. The duke was not as enamored with bluestocking ideas as she, apparently.

"Quite right." He nodded. "And perhaps Miss Charity will grace us with her singing at one in the not-too-distant future?"

His daring expression told Charity he knew exactly what he was doing.

"Oh, there is no need to hurt the ears of all and sundry." She shook her head. "Come now. How are you, my lord?"

"I am well. Aunt Victoria is here, in the corner. And we are bound and determined to enjoy ourselves at this smash."

"Excellent. And how is your aunt?"

"She fares well. I heard this morning that all her gout and other ailments of the nerves have bettered just in time to attend. I'm unsure how long she will last, but at any rate, she seems pleased to have come."

Charity never knew if Aunt Victoria's ailments were to be trusted. They were convenient to say the least. "I'm happy you could come." She eyed him, waiting, hoping for the usual first set which was well on its way to beginning.

But then he bowed. "Well, I am certain we shall cross paths again this evening." He turned to leave, and they were all aghast. Charity couldn't close her mouth at the surprise.

"What?" She swallowed. Lord Lockhart always asked her for the first set. In every ball they attended together he had raced to find her, no matter who surrounded her, and asked for the first set.

But right now, he walked away from them, nervously adjusting his sleeves. What had gotten into that man?

"I don't know what to say." She turned to the duchess.

"Nor I. Do you suppose he is intimidated by you?" The duchess looked her over. "He should be enchanted."

His Grace stood taller, his gaze traveling over the attendees. "Perhaps the lad is tongue tied. Happens to a man sometimes, you know, when the lady is particularly beguiling." The duke nodded as though an expert on the topic of amorous dealings.

7

"I cannot account for it." Charity watched him leave the ballroom, growing more puzzled.

Then a group of the more handsome set approached.

"Oh, dear." The duchess fanned her face. "They can have nothing to be interested in here."

"Except perhaps she will be all the more beguiling to the others of their sex who might have an interest." The duke nodded to Lord Granville who paused, greeted the duke and duchess, and then turned to Charity. "I did not know you would be in London for the Season." He dipped his head. "Might I have this first set?"

"Certainly. It's always good to see you, Lord Granville." They didn't always agree, but who *did* Charity always agree with?

As she placed her hand on his arm and he led her out onto the floor, he grinned. "I already know this set will be the most enlightening and lively in conversation of any I have of the evening."

She laughed. But only nodded.

"Come now, what is to be our topic? Wellington's last battle? The state of the poor and the cost of food? Or is it to be women's suffrage? Land ownership?"

She shook her head. "Have we already addressed all those issues, you and I?"

"We certainly have and more besides. You are an uncanny conversationalist. I only ask you for a set when my mind is up to it."

"And so you are energized and ready for a duel of words, then?"

"I am if you are so inclined, but might I say first, that you are particularly stunning this evening. I could hardly resist the set if my mind were mush."

She dipped her head, strangely flattered instead of offended at the mention of her beauty. "Thank you. Then perhaps we might discuss something that does not inspire debate?"

"Oh?" his eyebrow rose and the spark of interest in his expression told Charity that flirting might be easier than she imagined.

"Yes, I'd be most interested to hear of your estate. Your family. You."

He seemed flustered for a moment, but just briefly. "Well, I'm honored to have garnered a particular personal interest in one so well-read." He circled her in the set. "Then I shall tell you, all is well in the lake country. We do boast one of the prettier parts of England for my estate. Lakes, vales, flowers in bloom, plenty of rainfall." He paused. "And you? How are you and yours? The castle is well-nigh completed I've heard."

"It is, yes, thank you. We are all well. Mr. and Mrs. Sullivan are moved in to the castle and the stables have almost doubled in size." Charity shook her head. "Grace has opted to move to live with Lord and Lady Morley until her first season. And I move around between the two. Of course, now I am staying with the Duchess of York."

"Lovely people. He is also the man most apt to defend your causes on the floor of the House of Lords."

"Is he?" She turned to find her benefactor, but he had gone, the duchess deep in conversation with a group of her friends. "I did not know that." A man opposed to bluestockings but so open to change? She was intrigued.

"In truth, since talking to you, I've become much more inclined in the direction of universal suffrage. There is talk, you know, and of course the riots."

"And there you go, bringing up interesting topics. Shall we move on from the personal?"

"Are they not one and the same to you?"

She dipped her head in acquiescence. "I'm certain it seems as much." They moved down the middle of the line together. When they were facing each other again, she shook her head. "But tell me more of the lake country. I've never been."

She could hardly recognize herself. A perfect opportunity to cheer this lord on in his efforts in the House of Lords and she was bringing up the lake country? She couldn't account for it, except that she'd agreed to give this evening her best go at perhaps opening up personal connections with someone, more than one if possible. And, if she were being totally honest, she'd always wanted to see the lake district.

They talked of simple things, pleasant things; she learned all about his home. And by the end of the conversation, she felt almost as if she'd had a good coze. But she couldn't resist —as he was leading her off the floor, she pressed her hand into his arm for emphasis. "But I must tell you as well, I am most pleased with your efforts. If we can just get a large enough vote…"

He dipped his head back and laughed. "I didn't think you'd be able to resist. Yes, Miss Charity. You do not need to worry further. I have heard you and will do my best."

Only partly satisfied, she nodded. "Thank you, then."

"I *will* do my best. I take the role seriously, and knowing that I represent you gives me some motivation." He grinned and then straightened as though remembering himself. His bow was smart, and he left her just as another lord approached.

Charity danced every set with a different man, and no sign

of Lord Lockhart. Where had he gone? What was he up to? She eyed the door to cards, hoping he'd not succumbed to those trappings.

Finally, Lord Lockhart returned during supper. He was seated far from her, on the opposite end of the table, but their eyes met as he sat. He nodded once.

How mysterious. What on earth was going on with her friend?

She only half heard the conversation around her, aware more than ever of every laugh and feigned enjoyment from his end of the table. Until at last, when supper was over, she hoped he would come fetch her for a dance, but before she could say one word, he led another out onto the floor.

She froze in her steps. Would he go the whole of the ball without asking for a set?

He didn't look once in her direction and seemed as captivated as he ever was by the woman's conversation.

Charity shook her head and went in search of the duchess. Suddenly the ball in its entirety seemed tiresome. She hoped her steps were swift enough that even the bravest lords would not attempt to stop her in her path, but one moved to stand in front. Lord Wessex, in all his rakish glory, blocked her way.

"Excuse me." She tried to step around him.

"Oh, no, I'm pleased as anything you've crossed my path." He bowed. "Miss Charity. I've never seen you radiate so. I've been waiting for a chance to prove my dancing prowess. Would you please do me the honor?" His eyes widened, as though he didn't know every woman in the room pined for him. And then he tilted his head. "I do know you are much in demand and attempting to go elsewhere. I admit to hoping to dissuade that direction and distract you but for the time of this set?" His grin grew slowly, and she knew nary a woman would resist such a look and as it turns out, she was sorely tempted as well. At least perhaps Lord Lockhart might see her dancing and be reminded he could ask her himself.

His jawline was sharp, his teeth white, his breath, minty. "And we can discuss any number of things. I'm at your disposal."

And that is what cinched the deal. She laughed. "You've discovered a way into my heart it seems?"

When she placed a hand on his arm, his face, closer than she expected, grinned. "That is my very wish."

Her heart beat erratically before she calmed the ridiculousness. He was overwhelming in every way, but she must master her response to him.

The music to a waltz began, and while his grin grew, she tried to hide a groan inside. But he stood taller. "My luck is increasing by the moment." As he pulled her closer and his hand circled her waist, she knew she was in trouble indeed. Not for any minute did she think she might be caught in his snare, but he *was* certainly adept at winning a woman's affections and she was certainly not immune to them.

His eyes were the very shade of the Brighton seawater from the cliffs. His shoulders were broad and strong. Who knew she had a thing for jawlines? And his cravat touched his chin in crisp folds of white.

When she looked back up into his eyes, they were grinning back at her in amusement.

"You are a beautiful woman, Miss Charity."

"Thank you."

"And I love just looking at you. I'll be open and frank. You're stunning. Everyone in the room is watching, women, men, everyone. You've captured us one and all. And I am entranced." He led her expertly around on the floor.

She swallowed, unsure what to say or do in such a conversation.

"And I'm even more impressed as you refuse to simper and deny the hold you have on us."

She opened her mouth.

But he continued. "But here is my secret."

She waited.

He leaned closer, his breath tingling sensations down the soft skin on her neck. "I care less about capturing you for your beauty."

"Oh?" He'd certainly spent a good amount of words discussing something he now professed to care little about.

"I appreciate it, naturally. But you." His smile curled larger, then he leaned closer so that his mouth was hovering over her neck. "I want to win your *mind*." His lips brushed her ear as he spoke. Perhaps he'd done it on accident, perhaps on purpose, but she was struck by the wave of gooseflesh that jumped up along her skin.

"Oh?" She swallowed. Why could she think of nothing to say? Nothing at all?

"Certainly. You are my match in general appearance, but can I *impress* you?" He raised his chin. "I'm up for the challenge."

She had heard of this Wessex all over the ton. He swept through the women like a great tidal wave, leaving hearts broken in his wake. Just dancing a waltz with him would leave her open to discussion and speculation. The very last thing she needed was for him to enter some kind of quest to win her mind. "I hardly think that likely." She wanted to bite the words back as they left her lips, but there they were.

But he was completely unaffected by her not-so-subtle rejection. "I know you have a notion as to what I'm capable of already, but I shall prove you wrong. I shall prove"—he leaned closer again—"that I can be so much more."

He held her close as she danced in a circle at his side; they moved around each other in variations of the Waltz, her mind spinning with thoughts she could never say. How nice to entertain such a handsome man. But she knew, every part of her knew, he was up to no good. That as soon as he'd conquered her, the unconquerable, he would move on. And so she said nothing. And she determined that evening to spend time deciding what to say in just such a situation when her mind shut off. She laughed.

"Have I pleased you?" He smiled.

"Not precisely."

"Oh? And just what are you feeling, Miss Charity?" His finger, ever so subtly, ran a line down the bareness of her back.

"I'm feeling like you speak the truth. You are a handsome man, Lord Wessex. But winning my mind will be a challenge indeed."

She'd meant to dissuade him but instead, his eyes glowed with recognition. "One I can hardly resist. You must know."

And then she realized her mistake. The challenge was his greatest pleasure. "No, that's not—"

"Say no more. I shall show you by and by." The music ended, and he bowed. "That was a most informative dance. Thank you."

He led her to a frowning duchess, made his bows, and then moved across the room and out the door to the cards.

"Well!" The duchess fanned herself. "That was something to behold."

Charity clung to her arm for strength, to regroup. "What?"

"Your waltz. I've never seen such a sizzling pair."

"Sizzling?" She shook her head. "He has said he will not desist. He wants to win."

"Did he now!" She grinned, obviously thrilled with something. "This Season will be delectably entertaining and wildly successful, if that's the case."

Charity didn't know how that would possibly be the case. But she did know she was in desperate need of a lemonade. And a chair. "Do you think…" She looked around her.

Lord Lockhart joined them. "Would you like a lemonade? You must be positively parched."

"I am. Oh thank you, yes."

The duchess smiled kind eyes at him. "You have arrived at the perfect moment."

"Have I?" He looked from one to the other in some form of confusion.

"Yes, where have you been?" Her eyes turned to him, seeking answers, but he shrugged. "I've been here, same as you. Perhaps not dancing with half the ton." His eyes held more questions.

But she had no answers to give, and apparently neither did he.

"Can we get that lemonade? And then a chair? I might faint here and now."

"Well, none of that. No one has heard any of your treatises on the plight of the poor yet."

"No, they haven't."

"It has been an odd bit of a ball perhaps?"

"Certainly." She shook her head.

He seemed to be studying her more closely, but they made their way to the refreshment tables in silence.

The music began again. And once she'd downed the whole of her lemonade, he handed her another. But she now felt overheated. With her fan out, she looked about the room for a perhaps less crowded corner.

"Would you like to take a walk in the gardens?"

From anyone else, that would sound tempting in many ways, but from Lord Lockhart, it sounded like heaven. "Yes. Please. And perhaps there will be a bench, a nice, cool, secluded bench."

He raised an eyebrow at her. "Just what are you suggesting, Miss Charity?"

But he leaned his head back to laugh when she opened her mouth in shock. Then she swatted him and followed him through the ballroom, with more than a few looking on, out the back doors down the stone steps, and into the gardens.

With light strung up above, and a quiet space, the cool of the night air caressing her skin, she breathed out in relief. "Thank you."

"Of course."

He said very little, and their feet walked in silence on the soft padding of earth beneath. They passed through an entrance of hedgerows that guarded a squared-off garden space with a fountain and benches and roses to fill any romantic inclination.

She smiled. "This is lovely."

The bench did indeed feel cool on her skin, and Lord Lockhart was everything gentlemanly as usual. For once, his reticence to show emotion did not bother her at all. After the emotionally powerful Lord Wessex, Lord Lockhart was a soothing calm.

"I believe I've received some sort of odd proposal." He looked up to the sky, his face a mask.

CHAPTER 2

*C*harity choked. She couldn't stop herself. Everything had sucked in at such an alarming rate with his announcement that she didn't know what to do. She coughed and coughed until in some alarm, he handed her a handkerchief and pulled her to her feet.

He patted her back a moment, as gentle as can be—she hardly felt his hand—but her coughing continued and so he became more forceful until he hit one time with more serious intent and she felt somewhat relieved.

And then she started to laugh. With throat burning, eyes watering, and handkerchief to her nose, she laughed and laughed. "Oh Lord Lockhart. Thank you."

"You are quite welcome. I was concerned for a moment there that you might forever be coughing, but it seems you have recovered."

"Yes, quite." She wiped at her eyes. "But after that much needed laugh, I feel more like walking than sitting. Shall we?"

"Certainly." He held out his arm.

With her hand resting there, she felt a sense of wonder, of

being cared for, as though he offered his arm as a method of support and closeness. Perhaps the way it was originally intended.

They began at first in a circle around the small space surrounded by hedges. The sound of the water in the fountain filled the air around them and a faint scent of roses tickled her nose.

"How are the gardens coming at the castle?"

"Oh, what a happy turn of thought. They are beautiful. Lucy has turned out to be quite the horticulturist. She's secretly studied it for years and is pestering the gardeners with plans of her own. I've even seen her with dirt in her fingernails."

Lord Lockhart laughed. "Something I cannot imagine."

"No, not the old Lucy, but this version of my sister is the happiest. She seems in every way, free."

"That's excellent. A love match." He nodded.

"Yes, of course. You remember them at the wedding."

"I certainly do." He seemed distracted. And apparently he felt odd about something, because for a moment no one said anything, and it wasn't those delightful quiet moments where everyone is comfortable. It was one of those moments when thoughts filled the air as shouts but were completely unintelligible.

"So, are you going to tell me about this most shocking of all proposals?"

"I'm afraid to bring it up. At last mention you almost died in a fit of coughing."

"Never fear. I am quite recovered." She waited, growing more nervous as his face showed no sign of humor.

"Perhaps we can sit?"

"Certainly." She sat carefully, on the edge of the bench.

He pulled a letter from his pocket. "I received this yesterday."

And now Charity began to realize that he might be well and truly in earnest. "Who proposes to a man, and by letter?"

"I too am most confused." He cleared his throat, then opened the letter with unsteady hands.

My dear Wilfred,

Charity placed a hand on his arm. "That bears a moment of silence."

"What?" His mouth curved up, just at the edge.

"Your name." She shook her head. "You may proceed."

"Thank you. I don't know why my name is inciting this reaction."

"Oh just stop. Read on. I apologize."

My dear Wilfred,

Mother and I were just reminiscing this morning on that lovely afternoon when you and I were standing in the flowering trees. Well I remember the smell of the air with its hint of sweet and earth. And you earnestly declaring yourself. I have awaited anxiously the day when I can join you in London when we can show the world our long-held attachment, when I can at last be in all respects your intended as we once professed under the boughs of that tree. It sits outside my window and I think of you every day on my walks underneath it.

His hand dropped in his lap, letter still clutched. "She goes on, but that is the gist."

Charity at first did not know what to say. Did Lord Lockhart hold feelings for this woman? What was his declaration? Should she point out what she felt was obvious, that the woman seemed to be stretching the relationship and laying hold of a claim that might not be totally there? She watched his emotionless expression, uncertain what to say.

"For two years I've considered she and I a young flirtation, a time of great happiness between youths; at times I've even wondered what might occur between us. We did share expressions of the most amorous kind, as youth might when caught up in things. Neither were out in society. Neither of us anything but youth barely out of the school room. And I have felt some sense of responsibility toward her, to clear things before moving on, so to speak." His eyes flitted to Charity and back.

"But now. What am I to think? That I have inadvertently proposed to the girl?" He closed his eyes and for the first time, Charity noticed the pain that rested in their depths.

"Lord Lockhart, I hardly think—"

"And it doesn't signify does it, because if she's spoken of this? If there is an understanding? Won't she be quite ruined if I back away?"

Charity began to shake her head but then stopped. She didn't know. She was not privy to all the rules of ruination in the ton. She found half of them ridiculous.

"And so, that is why I feel unable to do much of anything to further my own happiness." The eyes he turned to her were full of hurt, sorrow, regret.

"But can you not simply reply with a brief, to the point letter explaining you are not under the same understanding as she?"

He turned away. "I do not know what to do. I have no one to advise me."

"And what about me? Am I not advising you now?"

"Of course." He placed a hand over hers. "But as you've said, you know as little as I about such things."

"Perhaps Gerald, or Morley." Both men in her life, a duke and an earl who had been her constant advisors. "Or the Duke of York. He has proven to be remarkably forward thinking."

"And do I need forward thinking? What if she is well and truly without recourse? We have been friends. We did in fact share a young relationship of sorts." He sighed.

"And this is why you did not ask me to dance?"

His gaze flickered to hers, in surprise. "I should never expect you to merely keep things unspoken."

"Of course not. What would be the point in that?"

"I don't know, to ease the way for others."

"Is this a difficult conversation? Is it not easier to simply say the truth and be done with it?"

"It depends on the listener and on the truth, doesn't it?" He looked away. "I don't have anything else to say on the matter as of yet. But I'm happy you know so there can be no misunderstandings."

Her heart pinched just a little bit. Was he saying they could have nothing between them? Did they not merit just as much of a consideration in his mind as this young girl from home? She shook her head. But at the sorrow in his face, she said no more.

Then she tugged at him, pulled him to his feet, and hugged him as tightly as she could. "I'm so sorry you are having to deal with this."

The arms that circled about her, at first hesitating, cradled her as though something precious, then his hands ran along her back and pulled her as closely as she'd ever been held. His heart hammered beneath hers, and she realized that she'd never hugged Lord Lockhart before.

Or if she had, it was never like this.

She clung to him, not knowing what else to do, but not

able to let go. She buried her head in his chest. "Lord Lockhart."

He rested a chin on her head and held her close, saying nothing.

When she pulled away, he wiped the moisture from his face quickly, but not quickly enough.

"What is this? Is this something you plan to take seriously? We can talk about this. You are not bound. We should speak with Gerald, certainly."

"No. I don't wish to speak to anyone, except you. The more who know, the more I'm bound." He adjusted his sleeve, an impatient, uncomfortable motion. "And shouldn't I be? If I left a young woman with the understanding that there would be more between us…what kind of man disappoints her?"

Charity wanted to shout all kinds of things about men and not pursuing something simply out of obligation, but she couldn't. She didn't know which one to say and she didn't dare say what was in her heart, which was a painfully obvious new realization that she didn't want Lord Lockhart pursuing anyone in the world, ever.

Except her.

THEY MADE their way back into the ballroom with nothing decided, nothing spoken, but everything seemingly changed.

The music to a waltz began, and Charity stepped into his arms. "Let's dance this set."

His eyebrows shot up to his hairline, but he nodded. "Certainly."

She knew he was reluctantly dancing with her. But he had sought to tell her his deepest concern. But she wasn't certain why. Did he plan to marry this girl from his past? Did he have feelings for Charity?

All their time together flashed before her eyes. All the moments of her great exasperation, every argument, every debate, every single time she'd taken him for granted and the regret that followed poignantly tore at her step by step as he attempted a semblance of indifference in their waltz.

But she could feel nothing but closeness.

And as she watched his handsome face, his deep brown eyes, try to avoid looking at her, she decided she was not giving up without a fight.

"I was thinking about the Corn Laws."

His eyes shot to hers. "You were?"

"Yes, what will happen to the poor in our country if they increase tax on corn? Who thinks of these things as any sort of solution?"

"They wouldn't."

"You said Lord Kenworthy mentioned it. Right on the floor of the House of Lords."

"Surely he was all talk. How could they do such a thing?" He shook his head.

"But do you ever wonder what it will take to keep the people from their riots? Perhaps we need to suppress them, keep books out of their hands, force them to spend all their energy working for their very subsistence?" She shrugged as if it were a viable option.

"No, Charity, are you hearing yourself? That is the worst idea. If we've dropped so low that we cannot trust our people to have intelligent thoughts, then we are low indeed." He began a lengthy discourse, quoting all of Charity's most favorite intellectual thinkers of the day until she was beaming, her mouth hurting form the force of such a large smile.

He stopped. "You did that on purpose."

"Of course. Someone needed to smack some sense back into your melancholy ways. Come, Lord Lockhart. Haven't we other things to be thinking of than your sorry swoony childhood love?"

"She's not my love. Childhood or otherwise." The gaze he sent piercing into her heart was adamant on that note at least.

She nodded, slowly, understanding somewhat. "All the better reason to shift our attention back to where it belongs, don't you agree?"

"I do, and I well remember we have a salon tomorrow. Perhaps we should bring up some of these very points. And after an excessive display like tonight, I'm of a mind to share with others less fortunate. How long has it been since we've offered food in South London?"

"Too long, I believe."

"Of course, last time you were almost accosted."

"But you came to the rescue."

"We shall have to come to some other arrangement."

"Can I not disguise myself?"

"You? And in what way do you think you could hide your beauty from a single soul?" He shook his head. "There is nothing for it. You shall have to watch from the carriage."

"I am certainly *not* watching from the carriage. Why even go, if I cannot assist?" And this banter, this familiar arguing with his adorably adamant soul felt more like home than anything else. Could things slip back to normal between them?

"You will watch from the carriage or dress like a man." He considered her. "And I don't even think that would help. Might make things worse."

She snorted. "Worse."

"Certainly, you don't think walking around in a pair of breeches is going to complicate things?" He turned a bit pink in the face. "Forgive me. I cannot even discuss such a thing without being wholly and inappropriately distracted." He stretched his neck against his cravat and held her at a greater distance.

She eyed him with pleased amusement. "I had no idea such a thing could be distracting."

"You are oblivious to many things."

She was about to be affronted, but the good humor in his face could not be denied and so she let it pass. "Then I'm happy to have you here to set me straight."

"Just so, but I don't believe your overly innocent face for one moment. You have no intention of listening to a thing I say no matter how right I am in my thinking."

"You never know. I could surprise you and pay a great deal of heed to everything you say."

"I don't know what I would do should such a day come."

"Likely faint."

He stood taller. "I would not faint."

"Fine. Perhaps you'd merely get a bout of the dizzy spells."

"Do you think so little of my manhood?"

"I think very highly of your manhood. It's what gets us into Whites and Boodles and at Jacksons and the races."

"Us. Us she says."

"Well, certainly. You go, and return and tell me all about it. How else are we to know which subjects to address to the mindless ton?"

"I don't think I'll ever know another way."

"There, see. We are the perfect team." She tapped his

nose, releasing him a moment in their dance. "Do you really think you'll ever find a better match?"

His gaze shot to hers.

"I mean, you know what I mean. Goodness, Lord Lockhart, all this talk of proposals has really flustered us, hasn't it?"

But his face turned serious, and he danced for many measures with a new intensity she didn't know how to counter, nor did she know if she wanted to. Thoughts of him considering honoring commitments to another were secretly warring with her peace.

When the set ended, he walked toward the duchess with a somber expression and when they were almost here, he said, "In answer to your question, no."

"No?"

"No, I don't think there will ever be a better match." He turned to leave but the duchess came forward and put both hands on his arm. "Oh, Lord Lockhart. Thank heavens you are here."

"What is it? How might I be of assistance?"

"It's the duke. He's lost terribly and is considering his cups. We can't have that, so I'm scurrying him home as though I'm about to faint from spells. But you, you need to see that Miss Charity gets home safely. Your aunt is here, is she not?"

"Yes, she is, and certainly. I will make sure she arrives home safely."

"Oh, you are a godsend." She looked over her shoulder and as soon as the duke came into view, she swooned with a hand over her head. "Oh goodness me."

Lord Lockhart leapt for her, holding her not-too-small frame in his arms and setting her upright.

"Good catch." She winked. "Oh, thank you. Thank you." She reached a hand to her head.

"What has happened? They summoned me." The duke frowned. "Are you well?"

"No. We must depart. Lord Lockhart is seeing to everything. Please, take me home."

His eyes grew tender, and he transferred her weight to his strong arms. "Certainly. Let us be off." He nodded to Lord Lockhart, took a long look at Charity, seemed satisfied with something and then the two left the room.

"Well, that was interesting." Lord Lockhart watched them go. Then he turned to her. "And awkward. When a man says something like I did, the hope would be to walk off immediately after, not have to face the subsequent conversation." His grin turned sheepish.

"Well, if you like, we can skip over the subsequent conversation."

His relief was tinged with disappointment, so she added, "But I was not asking merely in jest. I do think we are a remarkable team." She left it at that. Although appearing dissatisfied, he said no more.

CHAPTER 3

*L*ord Andrew Lockhart spent the rest of the ball in the company he most enjoyed. He and Charity likely disappointed the entire room full of eligible lords by not being available to dance, by walking the room, walking the verandah, walking the gardens, and sitting in the corner to enjoy another lemonade. He had no desire to do anything else or talk to anyone else. Now that he'd shared his dilemma from home, he felt free to be with her. He'd been given the express responsibility to see to Charity, and he would prefer that to all else anyway.

Would people talk? They might. But Charity had worked up such an odd reputation about herself they were likely to think he had intrigued her on some political subject. Which, he was proud to say, he had.

They were deep in a debate over whether the poor needed food or work when the final notes from the orchestra sounded, and Lord Lockhart realized that most people were leaving or had left.

His aunt approached, her sweet, tired face reminding him

of his duty there, and he immediately sprung to his feet. "Aunt Victoria. I am sorry. We lost track of time."

But she smiled and reached for him, her soft hand resting on his arm. "Don't think a thing about it. I was having an equally agreeable time of things and only just now noticed the hour." She smiled up into Charity's face. "And how are you, my dear?"

"I'm doing well, Lady Hackney."

The three made their way as slowly as Aunt Victoria's feet wished to lead them until they were at last standing on the front stoop, waiting for the Lockhart carriage.

As his aunt and her maid immediately fell asleep, and Charity sat as close as possible to him, her head on his shoulder, Andrew decided to do the least logical thing in the world and take the long way home.

Charity must have heard his instructions to the coachman and by her smile, he took that to mean she approved, or at least she didn't disapprove, for he'd surely hear her complaints if she did.

They drove around town, the dark of the early morning hours after a ball lending them silent streets and a full moon. He opened the window and looked out over her head.

"Lovely night," she murmured against his shoulder.

"It is indeed." He didn't dare take her hand. That felt more intimate than they should be. Her head on his shoulder could be a gentlemanly service as well as a friendly one. But hand holding, as much as he wanted those little fingers in his, was beyond what they were allowed.

For all these months, he'd kept himself in check, waiting for her to be ready, for her to realize just how suited they were, to see hints of her softening towards him…and then to receive such a letter from home. The timing could not be more terrible if he imagined up the worst possible scenario.

And so they drove. And he could tell by her shifting now and then that she was awake, but neither spoke. And something about the night felt magical as well as final. Was he saying goodbye to the potential between them? Was he holding out hope something could still work? He didn't know. So much had to be thought through. But regardless, he felt a poignant enjoyment in their experience.

A shout rang out in the street.

Charity jerked her head up and peered out.

He moved closer and gently tugged her back, hoping she was not in any danger. At any rate, it was better she not be seen at this hour in this part of London. They had strayed to the very edge of some seedy neighborhoods. "Let us both look," he joked, hoping he ignite her defenses against being told what to do.

A group of children ran through the streets.

"Are they playing? It's so late." She wrapped a shawl around her shoulders.

"Are you cold?"

She shook her head. "I'm fine."

They watched, and the children ran to what looked like a pile of rubbish on the corner.

"No." She shook her head.

They dug through it. The eldest held up the end of a loaf of bread. "There's more!"

The other children dove into the mess, rolling over each other to get to the bread.

"Oh dear no."

Andrew was so moved, he almost forgot about Charity.

His hand went out to hers—and not a moment too soon, as she attempted to open the door.

"No."

She turned to him in defiance. But he shook his head, inwardly pleading with her to see reason.

With no small amount of hesitation, she turned back to the scene which Andrew was equally entranced and saddened by. He hoped they would hurry past, but the coachman had slowed because the children seemed to dart here and there, and Andrew was equally glad he was being careful not to run over one.

A young girl approached the first boy, holding out her hand.

But he turned from her.

"What? No. That is too much." She reached for the door again.

Then the others started taunting her. "Oh, does Ronda want some bread?" They dangled their bits of rubbish in her face, and she began to cry.

Charity searched their carriage.

"What? What are you looking for?"

"Food. Any biscuits? Bit of something? She's starving. Our scraps would feed her."

He thought helplessly for something, anything, and then shook his head.

"We have to do something."

While he was distracted, she leapt down out of the carriage.

"Charity!" He leapt out after her, at a run.

She stepped over to the boys. "You stop that."

But Andrew arrived at her side before she could get too much farther. "Please. Get back in the carriage." His eyes travelled down the nearby alleyway. Men gathered on several corners. And one unsavory lot across the street were starting to take steps toward them. "We can come back. We have nothing. Let's come back when we can do something."

She shook her head.

But he turned her to face him. "Look at me. You know I care. I'm not discounting you. We *will* do something." He stared earnestly at her.

And she must have believed him because with one more look, she turned back to the carriage.

He hurried after her, almost picking her up, closing the door while the carriage took off nearly at a run.

"What on earth."

The group of men who'd been ambling over were now hurrying after. Some carried clubs. One lifted the girl up on his shoulders. The boys scattered.

"Oh dear." Charity shivered beside him. "Were they coming after us?"

"I don't know." He suspected they were. "I'm sorry to have driven this far out of the way."

She turned her brilliant eyes up into his face. "Why did you?"

She knew. She must know. Did she hope for a declaration? Her eyes were pools, and he wanted to be lost in them. He was helpless before her. He must tell her all. He could resist no longer. "Charity—"

His aunt sat up. "Andrew?" She peered out the window. "Good heavens! What are we doing here?" The alarm on her face reminded him of his reckless behavior. "I'm sorry, Aunt. We were taking the long way home, discussing our plans, and we lost track of time."

She settled back, obviously uncomfortable. "Let's hope we leave this part of town immediately."

The carriage turned. "I suspect James has that same goal in mind. Sorry to have concerned you, Aunt."

She didn't answer.

They continued on their way. Charity no longer sat as close. His aunt no longer slept. And he knew his moment had passed.

When they pulled in front of the duchess' townhome, the door opened immediately. And Charity hurried inside without a look back.

He and his aunt continued home to his smaller establishment. When they entered, the bleak emptiness of the place struck him. "Why don't we decorate, Aunt?"

"We could if you like. I've not had the funds until now." She patted his arm. "That Charity is a nice girl, isn't she?"

"Yes, she is."

She smiled, humming to herself. "Good night."

They parted ways, Andrew making his way to his warm bedchambers. If his home lacked furnishings, it did not lack in excellent help. The servants had a hot bath prepared, and he was soon relaxed and pulling blankets up to his chin in bed, a warming pan at his feet.

But he could not feel satisfied.

He had way more money than he would ever use. His estate raised more all the time. He would be leaving his heir and their children comfortable indeed. But his pillow felt uncomfortable for his head. The blankets were either too hot or too cold. He tossed and turned.

The solicitor informed him that another of his relatives had passed on and left the whole of their estate to him with a sizable fortune, as well as healthy functioning properties that produced a good amount each year. He must find a useful way to spend it, the surplus.

His money was being reinvested so as to produce more. He had wonderful financial advisors and his solicitor was most excellent. But he still had excess. His children would never want, but others?

He groaned, knowing he would be plagued forever by the young girl's wide blue eyes, by Charity's immediate reaction to her. Those children. He sat up. He was not going to sleep for many hours yet. He lit a candle, wrapped a rope around his now shivering self and sat at his table. With ink and quill, he started to write his concerns. He made a list of all the wrongs in his world that were associated with money. And then he started considering how he might or might not be able to assist with each one.

The candle burned on and he was still writing and thinking and considering. And by the end of it all, his candle was gone, and he'd come to only one solid conclusion: A conversation with Charity was necessary. She would know what to do.

With that, he at last fell asleep, knowing he would see her tomorrow.

Morning came quickly, earlier than anyone had a right to be up and about, but he called for his servant, dressed, ate a quick bite from the kitchen and made his way over to the York townhome.

No one seemed to be about—no walkers yet in the park across the street, no movement in the house, no horses—only the birds, the breeze and the sun barely rising in the sky over the horizon.

He didn't know why he thought he'd catch her early and he most certainly could not knock on the door. He turned from the knocker, having arrived close enough to see the coat of arms they'd added to the decor, and made his way back out onto the street.

But the door opened, and Charity stepped out. She was hardly dressed to be seen. But she looked as though she were sneaking. She had a bundle and a satchel, and she looked up and down the street before stepping out. As soon as she faced forward and almost stepped into him, she yelped. "Lord Lockhart."

She did not meet his eyes but seemed in too great a hurry for this hour of the day.

"Hello."

"Good morning. I think I shall be seeing you at the salon."

"Yes."

"It's not for several hours yet."

"Not for another five, certainly."

She nodded. "Are you here early? Or are you going for a walk very close to my door?" She adjusted the satchel on her shoulder and stepped further out into the street.

"I'm here early." He waited. But when she merely looked as though she would faint from not hurrying off, he took pity on her. "You're going to feed those children."

"I don't want to hear anything about it. They're hungry, and we have more than enough."

"I'm coming with you."

"What?"

"Certainly. But has it occurred to you that we don't know where they live or anything about them?"

"It has, yes."

"And you're still determined to do this today."

"I am."

"Excellent. Then let's find a carriage, shall we?"

"Where is yours?"

"Well, I think I left him over there." Andrew pointed back in the direction of the park.

She stepped up beside him. "You know, it's rather remarkable that you are here."

"I agree. And it's remarkable that you are thinking of precisely the exact thing I am thinking of."

"I am?"

"Yes, well, perhaps not precisely. But I've come early to talk to you, to ask your advice on how to best manage my affairs so that I might help with the poorer classes, with the children, all of it. I went over and over it all in my mind and by the end of it all, I determined only that the best first course of action would be to seek your counsel."

She stopped in her path and stared for a moment. In all his knowing her, he didn't think he had seen her speechless before. But she rallied and smiled. "Well, then let's get talking. We have food to deliver and a salon to host. No time to spend it discussing the weather."

"As if we ever discuss the weather." He snorted. "Can you imagine? It is rather lovely today, don't you think? Last night was freezing, even the warming pan—"

"Lord Lockhart."

He laughed. "Righto. So I have this detailed list." He pulled the folded paper he'd written last night out of his pocket.

"What is this?"

He felt suddenly very vulnerable in front of the woman who was adamantly always working on something to improve not just her life but all of England. He cleared his throat. "So what we have here is a list of all the things that could be improved with a little money."

Her eyes widened, and she leaned closer to look over his shoulder. The hint of mint filled the air around them. With a smile, he tilted the paper toward her so she could see.

At the top of the list, he had written about the children.

She ran her finger along the words. "Might I see this?"

"But if you hold it, then you aren't leaning over me like this. I quite like it."

She swatted him. "Oh stop. You will begin to sound like Lord Wessex."

He stiffened. "What do you know of Lord Wessex?"

"Not a thing except he is always on about …" To his great consternation, Charity blushed. "He's just the biggest flirt I've ever known."

"Not all flirting is rakish, of course."

She stopped and looked up into his face. "You are right. Some is quite welcome."

Before he could answer, she turned back to his paper. "Food, education." She nodded. "This is the problem."

"True." They approached his carriage and surprised a dozing coachman. When Lockhart told him their destination, the man looked as though he were about to complain, but instead he just nodded. "Yes, my lord."

"How will we be safe?"

"I'm not quite certain, but I think perhaps the street is safer in the day?"

She pressed her lips together. "How many footmen do you have?"

"Two on the back."

She rested a hand on her parcel and hugged her rucksack closer. "I hope to comfort, if even for a short time."

"I think you are most excellent for doing such a thing." He kept to himself his dismay that she was about to attempt such a delivery alone. Foolhardy would not even begin to cover how unwise it would have been. Even now, he questioned his own personal sanity.

"Education." She tapped her chin and then stared out the window.

"What are you thinking?"

"I'm thinking that things are pretty hopeless for everyone in that neighborhood unless they can somehow rise above their stations."

"And then what is available for them? And how does one do such a thing?"

"We saw it in Mr. Sullivan, didn't we?"

"But his situation is hardly the same, not with his own expertise and the attention from the crown..."

"How do you think he has become renowned with expertise?"

He considered her and then nodded. "By education. And then of course from noble attention."

"Right. I think there is perhaps a way we can help here."

"With education?"

"And food. What if we opened a school?"

He should have known that involving Charity would be a full commitment and an involved one. But that was what he wanted, wasn't it? "Could we do such a thing? What know we of schools?"

"We are educated. We know how to read. That alone might lift these beggarly children out of the gutter."

The truth of her words hit home. "I hear you, and I think this is a great idea. I have no idea how to accomplish such a thing, particularly in the neighborhood where the most need exists."

"We can talk to the others about that. With all of us thinking together, surely we will find a way."

She seemed so sure of herself. She seemed to know it was going to work out before they'd even planned a single particular. Charity Standish was a singular woman. "You. Are one of the smartest people of my acquaintance." He grinned, suddenly so proud of her he wished to tell others.

But instead of glowing under what he assumed would be her hope of highest praise, a flicker of uncertainty crossed her face. But then she smiled. "Thank you." She peered out the window. "We're getting closer."

The roads became more crowded. Carts with people selling any manner of things, the smell of rotted vegetables, the noise of shouting and loud laughter all alerted them to a different lifestyle than they were accustomed.

As Charity watched for a moment, she shook her head. "I'm no different from any of them."

"What? Of course you are."

"But in what manner? Right now I have everything, but in the past, I have had nothing—no income, no hopes for more, nothing."

"But your connections, your... education, deportment, language. Yes, I see. That is what set you apart from them."

She nodded and looked back out the window. "How will we ever find her?"

"Are you looking for that one particular girl?"

"Yes. I just want to reward her plumb. And her courage. I want her to know she's not alone."

"We're approaching the alleyway where we were last night."

She poked her head out and when eyes started looking

their way, focusing in on her, he wished she wouldn't, but he didn't say anything.

He was happy to support her and wanted this to be just as she'd hoped. They could discuss future safety particulars on the way back to the duchess' home.

CHAPTER 4

*C*harity could not believe her luck. She had marched out of the house with her gifts and no idea how to accomplish her goal. But she'd wanted to help that girl, to give her some hope. And of course, food. Perhaps a hired hack could have taken her. Perhaps she would have had to go begging in the duchess' stables for a ride. She really hadn't thought it through, but it was early enough in the morning, she had given herself many hours to figure it out.

And Lord Lockhart had been on her doorstep, with a carriage.

A figure darted in between and around the people and carts pushing forward on the street sharing space with their carriage.

"There." She looked closer.

Lord Lockhart leaned closer, his face beside hers now, peering outside. She breathed in the smell of him. Mahogany and leather, comforting her and strengthening her. They'd done a lot together. They could figure this out. She squinted. "There again."

The girl looked to be playing in the street. She darted here and there, bumping some and nearly toppling over others.

"I think she might be stealing." He frowned.

"No. Is she?"

They watched her for a time, and after a while saw patterns. If she wasn't stealing, she was certainly doing something, and with a purpose.

Charity was disappointed. She'd hoped the girl was without fault, abused by her environment and simply two steps from starvation.

"The man is making her."

She followed Lord Lockhart's gaze to the same man who had put her up on his shoulder last night. He stood in a corner and accepted something from her now and again.

"The most devilish practice." She was sick inside, for the young girl, for the world she lived in, for all of it.

"How are we going to get her our gifts?" Charity didn't want her to have to give up the food to anyone else.

"Do you still wish to give them to her?"

"Certainly. You don't think that just because she's doing something wrong, something that is likely paying for her food, that I would refuse to help her?"

He held up his hands. "I'm saying, will she get to keep anything you give her?"

As they watched the girl run by the man again, depositing more into his hands—which he stuffed in the bag on his shoulder—she realized the truth of what he was saying reflected her own fears.

She wanted to help that girl. More than anything, she just wanted her to have a bite to eat. Charity jumped out of the carriage.

And Lord Lockhart followed right after.

Every eye on the street noticed them. Most pretended to still be about their activities but Charity felt a very real scrutiny.

The young girl ran toward them, but before she could get close enough to bump into her, Charity slipped a biscuit in her hand.

The girl stopped, almost tripping up. "What's this?"

"I remember you, from last night. You asked for a bit of bread."

Her eyes widened. "You came back." She looked from her to Lord Lockhart. "To give me food?" Her eyes narrowed.

The man in the corner stood taller, watching them.

"Eat it. It's yours." Charity smiled. "I have more. Are you hungry?"

The girl almost swallowed it whole and so Charity shared cheese with her next. And then another biscuit.

"If I give you more to take with you, will you have to give it away?"

Her face filled with fear and she ran.

Charity walked through the crowd, handing out some of Cook's finest morsels until her satchel was empty, and they returned to the carriage.

On their return to the duchess' townhome, they said little. Her mind was racing with thoughts, plans, hopes, logistics. But after a moment she sat back in frustration.

"I don't know the slightest thing about running a school."

"Nor I. But I've been to one, so that helps somewhat perhaps."

When they arrived, she waved him in. "You must join us. We have preparations for the salon to complete, but perhaps after, with a few remaining friends we can discuss more about the school."

He followed her into the house. The smells of breakfast filled the air, and his stomach rumbled.

"We might take the morning meal as well. Come." She led him into what looked like a smaller dining room. Breakfast was set up on the side table and the duke sat with multiple papers and flyers on the table in front of him.

"Good morning, Your Grace." Charity curtseyed. He was a dear man, no matter that he complained of her blue influences on the duchess.

He lifted his eyes and then his eyebrows as he eyed Lord Lockhart. "Lockhart." His tone a greeting, a question and a warning all in one; the man knew how to act in his station, certainly.

"Your Grace." He bowed.

"Lord Lockhart is here for breakfast and to aid with the salon we are hosting."

"I'll be making my way to Whites. You're free to join me if you like." He went back to reading his paper. Charity smiled to see the latest Whims and Fancies column on the back of the page he was reading.

"Kate's been writing about gloves of late."

"Oh?"

"Yes, she's determined that more color make an appearance."

"And when she writes something, people take heed?"

"Oh certainly. It helps that she has an excellent eye and consults with the modiste often. She has an understanding of the styles and how they change." Charity was proud of her sister. She herself could have never taken that path, but she'd been blessed by both her knowledge of fashion and her excellent cheerful outlook about the sisters' situation in society. "I miss Kate."

"Is she coming today?"

"Yes." Charity grinned. "June, Kate, and Lucy will all be here."

"And not their husbands?"

Charity frowned. "Often I can get Logan. He is very forward thinking in his work in the House of Lords, and we discuss and support his latest bills in the salon. But I don't know if he will be here today. I haven't heard. The others? I can only guess." She turned to him. "As you've experienced, these meetings attract more women than men."

"I'm happy to at least represent my sex."

The duke grunted. "Like I said, you are welcome to join me at Whites." He turned the page of his paper.

"Thank you, Your Grace."

He didn't answer.

Lord Lockhart sat beside her as they took their breakfast. How companionably pleasant to share such a simple activity. How nice would it be to do so often with such a man.

She couldn't believe the direction of her thoughts. When had she ever considered life with a man? Never, really. For most of her younger years, when they'd had nothing, when all five sisters still lived together in their cottage, she'd thought the opportunity to marry would never come. She'd happily sat back hoping one of the other sisters would have a chance and suspecting she might never attract a man. It was quite freeing to say whatever she liked and do whatever she liked.

But then she'd found great satisfaction in the learning and conversations and the change that could happen around them. She found that she could make a difference simply by speaking her mind. She'd discovered that much was wrong in their world. And she had been full of fire to be someone who would spark the change.

But now, with the other sisters marrying one by one, and now that she knew everyone had a chance to marry, she'd been concerned that she'd become too obviously focused on other things, that men would not even know how to approach her amorously.

And that's when Lord Lockhart had captured her attention.

But she had no idea what to do with her feelings, especially since he'd told her of a possible responsibility for a woman back home. That seemed like a difficult obstacle for them to overcome if they were to ever be together. And the man likely viewed her as a companion in their work and nothing more. She'd never met someone so wholly focused on doing good with what he'd been given.

They ate quietly for the most part, now and again engaging the duke in conversation.

His Grace left soon after.

When the door closed after him, Charity held out her hand. "Let's see this list of yours."

He unfolded the paper and placed it between them.

His closeness, the goodness of his heart, the fact that he'd created such a list at all, reminded her how much she respected him.

She reached for her tea and their hands brushed, sending tingling awareness through her. She'd become accustomed to such waves of sensation and would have ignored them except that Lord Lockhart paused as well, and there was this space between them that felt full, and warm and charged with something...intense. The very air between them brought them closer, but not close enough. And so the feeling continued. And intensified. Until she rested her hand on the table, and he placed his beside hers. The space between the two but the breadth of a spoon. She sat very still, the anticipation of his hand near hers, the thought that he might move, just an inch, to touch her, grew and strengthened until when the door opened, she jumped.

"Goodness. Are you all right, my dear?" Her Grace nodded to them both as they stood when she entered.

"Oh, yes. You startled me."

"I see that." Though she surely had suspicions, she said nothing more and filled her plate.

"Are you looking forward to the salon, Your Grace?" Lord Lockhart seemed perfectly in control of himself, at least his voice sounded placid and normal.

Charity as yet did not trust herself to speak.

"Lawrence Hamilton is one of the great minds of our day." The duchess sat across from Lord Lockhart. "When he has finished his presentation, I'll have a considerable amount of questions to ask him."

"Oh? What shall be your first?"

"Where has he been for the past fifteen years?"

"Has he disappeared?" Charity was now intrigued enough to recover her faculties, somewhat.

"He *was* a big name, spoke often at salons and things when I was younger, during an earlier wave of bluestockings, but he has been silent for many years. And I for one would like to know what he's been up to." She sipped her coffee. "I hope he's been practicing all those things he used to say with such power and emotion. I hope he's been building schools and working for the poor and helping equal out some of our separation of wealth."

Charity and Lord Lockhart exchanged a hopeful look.

"But I suspect he has not, else we would have heard of such an effort?"

"Who's to say until we ask him, Your Grace." Charity

placed her fork on her plate. "We have just now been talking about schools. The poor. How can they rise above their misery without knowing how to read or calculate? Knowing those two things would surely be life altering."

"Surely. If I were younger, those are the kinds of things I might become impassioned about. Consider all a person could do if he or she were allocated time and resources."

"Your Grace. If we were to find a way to begin a school, could we count on your support?" Lord Lockhart asked with a smile, but his sincerity beamed out of him.

Charity was amazed at his boldness, the direct question and then even more so that the duchess nodded. "I would, depending on the efficacy of the venture. I would want to know all the details."

"We shall express them as we have them. Your input would be gratefully welcomed also."

"I shall do my best, naturally. I find, though, that my best contribution is simply my acceptance. My hosting the salons and participating in the talks."

"Certainly. Your support has empowered so many more to brave censure and assist in all manner of causes."

"And why should they have to brave censure? What a skewed society we live in that shames intelligence and decries assistance to the poor."

Charity reached a hand over to cover the duchess'. "I shall remember your kindness forever."

She waved the gratitude away, but Charity knew she was touched.

After breakfast, she and Lord Lockhart met in the front drawing room with paper and quills and began to consider all viable options. They would have something to present when they first mentioned the idea before their group of friends.

Charity hoped that in some way, she could help the children, that she could also feed them. Surely they would have baskets of sustenance to offer. In all things, she wished to take away the pain and injustice she'd seen in the life of the one brave little girl running around the streets in the South of London.

CHAPTER 5

*B*y the time the guests started to arrive, Andrew had at least some place to start with their plans to try and run a school for the poor of London. He laughed to himself.

He knew a few had sponsored schools in the villages close to their estates. Such a thing was not unheard of. But in London, with children from the poorest families? They might need to begin with a different group in a different location.

Louder than usual happy greetings sounded from the front door.

The Standish sisters had arrived. He grinned and made his way to witness the exuberance.

Arms and dresses and all manner of kisses in a great flurry filled the area in front of the door. Every sister, as radiant and beautiful as the next, but none so much as Charity. She usually kept her affection restrained, except when with her sisters. Watching the joy light up their faces was a beautiful sight indeed.

They turned to face him all at once and then the focus of

their great joy in gathering had turned to him. "Lord Lock-hart!" Kate approached with a curtsey. As he took her hand and then all the others in turn and bowed before them, his smile only grew.

"Our loyal male representative." Lucy shook her head. "The others should be here."

"Certainly. If all men could just be like our loyal Lord Lockhart." June sighed.

"Oh stop. We mustn't act as though he's our token man." Charity moved to stand beside him. "There are others, certainly."

Charity placed her hand on his arm and the group moved into the parlor where chairs had been set.

"This is lovely." Kate turned approvingly.

"Thank you. The duchess is all kindness and quite impassioned by the cause herself."

They stood in a small group, partway into the room and Andrew listened while the sisters

caught up on each other's lives.

"Julian is as good a baby as any I've seen." June smiled. "We are blessed."

"She hardly lets the nursemaid have a moment with him." Lucy laughed.

"And how is the castle?"

"The renovations are complete. The old artifacts and scrolls and history is being

considered by experts. And some of it will become part of a museum collection." Lucy smiled. "The rest of it will be on display in a new room we have dubbed the Standish O'Sullivan

personal museum. And we are carefully preserving and putting on display some of the featured pieces, the armor, the suit of arms, the O'Sullivan ring, the rattle." Her face lit with excitement.

"I will invite you all down for an extended stay when the room is complete. We must celebrate."

Andrew watched them talking and wished more than anything to be a part. He had so

little by way of family; the Standish sisters seemed to have it all. They loved and laughed, and he already knew how fiercely they defended one another. What did he have left? His dear Aunt Victoria. And grateful he was for her.

While his eyes hungrily drank in the feelings of love and family that surrounded him, he knew he could start working on his own at any time. Charity laughed louder than the others in a beautiful and unrestrained way. Was he working on his future family already?

Thoughts of Penny and her mother and the years when they were his family nudged his sense of gratitude and responsibility. He had more than he gave himself credit for having. And it would do him good to remember.

But Penny and her family had nothing like what the Standish sisters had. No joy. No unity that he ever noticed. No love.

He'd thought there had been love between he and Penny. But after knowing Charity, after seeing more of the world, he knew that what he'd felt with Penny was perhaps but a need to assuage his loneliness, a companionship when they'd both needed someone.

But he had moved on to more and better while she had not. She was still there, in Buckinghamshire, with her family…such as it was.

Charity stepped closer and squeezed his arm in her hands.

"I apologize. I'm woolgathering. What have I missed?"

They laughed and June shook her head. "We have been rhapsodizing over your great efforts to help in the cause. Charity just mentioned a school now, too?"

"Oh yes. Those ideas are as new as any we've had. I hope you can linger after to help us work through some of the specifics?"

"Charity's already roped us in. We will be there." Kate laughed.

"She ropes in everyone eventually. It's the Charity way, there's no resisting her." Lucy had seemed to grow in appreciation for her sister as the Season progressed last year. Andrew was relieved she'd married who she did. Though he had no business having a preference one way or another, he greatly preferred Mr. Sullivan.

The room filled with guests. He took his seat on the front row next to Charity, who would be conducting the meeting.

And still no sign of Mr. Lawrence Hamilton.

Andrew took the small pocketsize book of essays out of his jacket.

"I didn't know you had that." Charity tried to read over his shoulder, so he moved it closer to be shared between them.

"When I heard he was a favorite, I ordered it straight away."

She shook her head. "You are maddening at the same time you are impressive, my lord."

"And why are you my lording me?" He narrowed his eyes in suspicion.

"I didn't notice that I was." She turned to the door. "What if he doesn't come?"

The room was full. The conversation had hushed. It was time to begin, and everyone was waiting.

"We shall just have to stall." He sat up, about to stand and do the craziest thing he'd yet done.

"What are you doing?"

"I have his words. Perhaps we shall read some?"

"Can you do readings?" Her eyes widened, the hope that lit in them gratifying him to no end.

"Well, I can read." He laughed as he flipped to his favorite of the essays.

She placed a hand on his arm to stall him and stood up herself.

"And now, ladies and gentlemen. We are so grateful you have joined us this evening to hear the words of Mr. Lawrence Hamilton. He has been delayed but we will begin the program with the hopes that when his slotted time arrives, he will be here to address us."

And just like that, she smoothed over the awkwardness of their beginning.

She squeezed his hand as they passed each other, he moving to stand in front of a rather large group, and she returning to her seat.

He cleared his throat. Some of society's highest born ladies were present in this room along with the members of their typical group. The duchess' influence was useful indeed. He remembered that Mr. Hamilton had been a leader in the original groupings of the bluestockings. Perhaps all of these ladies had been a part.

The wife of an extraordinarily pompous earl spoke next. "At last, the return of Mr. Hamilton. I too am anxious to meet the man, to hear where he's been."

A low murmur of agreement moved through them.

"I respect his words. And I ask myself, just as I'd like to ask him, where are the actions to back the sentiments? We have high thoughts, high hopes, much moralizing as regards to the plight of the poor, but what are we doing about it?"

Andrew cleared his throat, ready to begin. Charity's eyes were shining in happiness, his words being her very thoughts on the matter he knew, yet the others might not be as prepared to hear them. "With those thoughts to nudge us, I will begin with his essay titled, 'Sentiments on the Plight of the Poor.'"

He'd quite enjoyed the man's words and so reading aloud with feeling and emotion came naturally. He was lost in the treatise itself until the end. When he read the final line, and the ladies all clapped, he blinked in surprise.

Had Mr. Hamilton arrived? Charity shook her head.

"Shall we move on to perhaps his most famous?"

Andrew read and read, entertaining as best he could. The ladies laughed and wiped a tear or two. Perhaps he'd done the man's ideas justice. He hoped he'd helped Charity's event be successful. At the finish of the next essay, he closed the book. "And so must begin our discussion. Who has had thoughts right now, during this salon, of ways you could make a difference?"

For a moment, no one said anything at all, and Andrew worried he'd just created a long awkward silence, but then the Duchess of York, seated in the back, stood. "I've spent the last fifteen years of my life thinking on those days of our first bluestocking meetings. I've known we had good ideas back then. I've reviewed my notes and I've not done what I could. Listening again from the mouth of this powerful orator, I know I can do more. Who will pledge to act?"

The ladies nodded and murmured in agreement. Another woman raised her hand. "I too, feel called to do something, but what?"

The Duchess of York winked at him.

Charity joined him at his side. "We have an idea."

"Just today we came to an important conclusion."

Then Charity outlined their thoughts on a school. "But there are some complexities to work through and for this, we could use your help."

"For example. Where in London would be a useful and safe place to hold a school?"

The women hummed in excitement. Many erupted in conversation with those at their sides. They had not planned to bring the whole group into their planning, but it had seemed the perfect moment. Lord Lockhart winked back at the Duchess of York.

"How about a church? I think there are areas just north of London with a vicar or two who could assist us." The speaker was an elderly lady dressed with more ornamentation than the rest of them. Andrew didn't know who she was, but Charity placed a hand on his arm. "Oh, Lady Everly. That is an excellent idea. I wonder if even perhaps some churches closer, like Saint Paul's for instance. Would they be willing to open their doors, their offices or their classrooms as a service to the poor among us?"

Lady Everly nodded. "And if anyone needs to speak to these men of God, I'll be the first to remind them of their duties."

With the support of such a highly respected member of their party, the other women in the room started calling out ideas as well. A servant brought paper, an inkwell and a quill, and Charity took furious notes. By the time they were finished, the plans for a school were in place, the funds were allocated, and several promising locations were about to be researched. Charity looked as though she might be walking on the clouds.

And then a man entered the room; the servants announced him as Mr. Lawrence Hamilton. Every head turned around to see a stranger sway in place, obviously in his cups, a crumpled piece of paper in his fist, his hair disheveled, his suit coat old and thread born, and a sneer on his face. "You think can change any of this? Do you think your small ideas will actually make a difference?" His hand gripped the back of the nearest chair.

The women in the room leaned away from him, several with handkerchiefs to their noses.

"I've been here. I've been to these salons. We talked like we knew what was best. We made plans. We wrote essays." His hand indicated something about Andrew. "But what good did it do? What change did we make?"

The rising panic in Charity's eyes urged Andrew to action. He moved to the back of the room toward Mr. Hamilton. And then the Duchess of York stood. Her servants entered the room and looked ready to take action if necessary. Andrew raised a hand toward Mr. Hamilton in what he hoped was a calming gesture. "We were just talking about where you have been. Your words inspired a whole room of powerful women to make a difference. They each remember your stirring causes. Good can happen. Change can come."

"I used to think so too." He swayed. "You'll see. All of you will see how pointless it is when there's so much that is wrong around us."

"Thank you for your thoughts. I believe we have a basket for you in the study." Andrew looked over his shoulder and shrugged.

Charity nodded, and he was certain they had something as a thank you gift for the man, and it was pretty apparent he needed to leave.

"Trying to kick me out? Think you can come in, read my words, and then kick me out?" He stepped closer as if to confront Andrew but then he moved like he would push his way to the front and have words with all the women.

"I'm sorry you're late. We all are, but we were just wrapping up. Maybe next time. Everyone here would like to know more about you and what you've been doing."

"I'm here now." He stood taller. He looked like he would try to keep walking, perhaps through or around Andrew.

Andrew stood in his path. They were about the same build. Mr. Hamilton stood at eye level with him. And he swayed, unsteady. Andrew didn't relish fighting, but if it came to that, he could get the man out of the room. He nodded to the footmen who approached.

Mr. Hamilton whipped around and then back to face him. "Throw me out?"

"No, certainly not. Just to show you where we've placed your coat and basket. We're so glad you have come." He stepped closer and clenched his fists, ready.

Mr. Hamilton turned red in the face and he stiffened. For a moment, Andrew thought he was going to throw the first punch, but then he backed away. "Where did you say they put my things?" When he turned, a footman stood on each side of him.

"The butler will take good care of you."

The duchess had been in whispered conversation with one of the servants. As soon as Mr. Hamilton was out of the room, the double doors were shut, and two other footmen stood in front of them.

"My, my." Charity stood up at the front again. "That was unexpected." She looked as flustered as Andrew had ever seen her.

Andrew clapped his hands once for attention. "We will just give Mr. Hamilton time to collect his belongings and then we can move to the refreshments, and those of you who are staying to join our committee for the new school can begin that very quick meeting."

For the most part, the ladies looked disturbed. Fans were out. Whispers were going. And Andrew wondered if they should just end the evening early with hopes to reconvene.

But the Duchess of York moved to the front of the room. "And now we know."

The whispers stopped. Eyes turned to her.

"Now we know what Mr. Lawrence Hamilton has been doing all these years." She laughed.

And others joined in.

"And perhaps this shall be a lesson to us, to not let another year go, waiting for someone else to make something of themselves, for someone else to lead out. We can do it ourselves."

The fans lowered and here and there, a woman nodded.

Charity's face filled with relief.

Eventually, the footman gave the signal that all was clear. The guests could have refreshment. But not many lingered. Everyone expressed a desire to help with the school. They murmured their commitments as they walked past Andrew, getting their things from the butler and being handed up into their carriages.

But Andrew couldn't blame them.

When everyone had gone, Charity stood beside him. "Do you believe them to be sincere?"

He nodded. "I do. I think that Hamilton fellow—dash it all —put a damper on things, but I am certain they wish to help. I'm certain that a school is a splendid idea, and I even approved of our locations."

They walked together back to the front sitting room and fell onto the nearest sofa.

"We act as though we've hiked for many miles."

"I feel as though I have."

"But you were brilliant." She closed her eyes and rested her head on the back of the sofa. "If I were not so tired, I'd tell you with more energy."

"I like this best I think."

She opened one eye. "This semi-conscious version of me practically sleeping on the sofa?"

"Yes, exactly this version. The one where you've spent your entire day doing good, so much so that you are now spent." He leaned his head back. He had to scoot rather a large amount forward so that his head could rest on the sofa but once he'd accomplished his new posture, he closed his eyes.

"What do you think?"

"Dreadfully uncomfortable."

"Naturally for you." She shifted beside him. "But this is quite lovely for me."

He sat back up quietly so as not to disturb her, for she looked even more stunning in such a perfect repose. He lifted her hand in his. "Think what these hands have accomplished today. You smuggled food from the kitchen, snuck out of the house, bent on making a delivery to a seedy neighborhood in the South of London."

She smiled.

"And then these hands hosted a reading salon where the actual guest never showed up until the end when he made a spectacle of himself because he was in his cups."

She frowned.

"And throughout, in bits and pieces, you planned the

building of a school and the education of London's poor." He laughed.

"Seems like quite a lot."

"Yes it does."

"Sometimes I like to just be a regular person."

Nothing could have surprised him more, but he said nothing, hoping she'd explain.

"I'd like to go to a ball, dance just for the pleasure of it, be courted by men, talk only of simple things, like the weather, and be seen as…" She opened her eyes.

He was struck by the brilliance that stared back at him.

"Be seen as truly a woman."

He started to tug off her gloves. "I can't think properly when your hands are covered."She laughed. But her eyes widened enough that he knew he had her attention. Her complete attention.

As soon as her bare hand was in his, he marveled at its softness. "Much better."

"Mm."

"Miss Charity." He lifted her hand to his lips. "No one would see you as anything but one of the most beautiful women of their acquaintance."

Her cheeks colored prettily and as much as he adored the intelligent Firestarter Charity, he was drawn to this new tender side to her.

"But you should have heard Lord Granville."

"Lord Granville?" He tried not to be shocked by the abrupt entrance of another lord in the middle of one of the most intimate conversations he'd had with her.

"Yes. I had to basically explain that I wasn't interested in talk of political change before he would move on to the more typical subjects."

"I bet he was as disappointed as I would have been."

Her eyes held sorrow, and he regretted his words. "What is it? People love your conversation."

"I know."

"And they love you too. It's all one package. You're everything—the mind, the humor, the beauty…" He needed to be more mild in his compliments, especially since he hadn't yet written home and he didn't at all know what the expectations were from Penny. But Charity was the most amazing woman he'd ever met, and suddenly he was filled with desire that she know it.

"But what if it's time for me to…consider this Season as more than a means to help solve England's problems? If I wish to meet others and dance and discover perhaps…someone." She lifted her lashes to his, and the implications of her words shook him. "You wish to marry?" Hope and fear raged through him in equal amounts.

"I think so? Those are fearsome words to speak. I would never have said them but since you have, I can acknowledge that all these years I'd thought to never marry, and now that I know the opportunity is before me, I fear I've pushed away any real chances because of my uncensored speech."

He held her hand in between the two of his own. "Never censor your speech."

"Oh, you say that." She pulled her hand away to wave it in the air. And then began tugging off her other glove. "Of course that is how you feel. I've only ever known you as a brilliant partner in all of these efforts. But the others? They might not wish to hear so much from me. You should have seen Lord Fallon's reaction when Lucy finally spoke her mind." Charity shook her head, obviously annoyed.

"But you don't need to concern yourself with curbing your tongue. Everyone quite enjoys it."

"Perhaps as a form of entertainment, or as an engaging conversation, but how often have I heard warnings about curbing my tongue or I'd never find a man?" She sighed. "Don't listen to me. I'd never be able to give it up even if I tried. I just worry about what I'm sacrificing."

"And you'd like to start a family?"

"I would, yes." She shrugged. "As silly as that sounds."

"It doesn't sound silly at all." He studied her for many minutes, until she once again closed her eyes. Her breathing steadied and he realized that her talk was from a delirious, overly tired brain and anything he said might not really penetrate her consciousness.

Then he stood. "Let's get you up and moving so that you can climb those stairs and get yourself some sleep."

"We have a big day tomorrow."

"Tomorrow? I thought we weren't meeting until Friday."

"That far away? Why not tomorrow?"

"Perhaps the both of us could use some rest?" He also had a visit with his solicitor to make and a letter to write.

"I suppose."

He walked her out of the room and toward the staircase. "Thank you for today. I believe we shall do good together with this. The school was an excellent idea."

"Thank you. And thank you for being here, for your rescue two times today."

"You're welcome."

She turned from him, barely able to walk, let alone think straight.

He watched her all the way up the stairs, and then he turned in the direction of the front door.

The duchess surprised him when she stepped out from one of the rooms.

"Thank you, Your Grace." He bowed. "I appreciated very much your words today."

"Oh tosh. It is only the truth I speak. More importantly, how are things with Charity?"

He laughed nervously. "Do you mean am I pursuing her?"

"Yes, precisely, obviously you're pursuing her, but how is the pursuit? Perhaps some success today?"

Andrew smiled uncomfortably and made a short bow. "I could not say."

"I shall know just by looking at you both. If you won't tell me, I have my ways."

"She's lovely. I don't know if she wishes my pursuit of her or that of another, but I pray it is me she wants in her life." As long as he was free to pursue her.

"Very good." The duchess seemed to be thinking about something but then shrugged it off, and Andrew knew he would never know.

He took his bows and was soon in his own carriage on his way back to his empty house.

CHAPTER 6

*T*he next morning, he bid his solicitor goodbye just as a servant brought in the mail tray.

Andrew waved him forward. "Thank you, Timothy."

When he glanced at the letter, he wished to hand it back. All this recent progress with Charity brought his behavior in question now that Mrs. Westchester was writing him. Thoughts of Penny, her written acknowledgement that they had said things to each other as youth, that he'd made promises, made him wish to toss this letter without opening it. But he knew it was time to face this responsibility, to determine just exactly what his relationship with the family should be, and address it head on.

His finger slid under the seal, breaking it in two. "And here we go."

He unfolded the papers, surprised at the length of the letter. Fanning out the parchment, he was looking at a six-page double sided letter, some from Mrs. Westchester and some from Penny.

He sighed. They had much to discuss and attempt to

understand. Her mother began with several pages of memories she had of him as a child. And without meaning to, Andrew slid into a happy train of thought about all the times he'd found happiness in an otherwise bleak upbringing. All moments of happiness had been with the Westchester family.

Andrew remembered a particular morning, his tutor had been frustrated, his mother not available to him. He didn't know what she was doing, but he remembered being told not to disturb her. And then his father came in, likely at the behest of his tutor.

"Son. I understand you are not learning the material."

"It is just this one part…"

"All the parts must be learned. Your tutor has suggested a school that might assist."

"What? I don't want to go to a school. That's why we're doing tutors. I thought we talked about this."

"Perhaps if you apply yourself, we can avoid sending you away, but it is nothing to dread. I enjoyed my days at Eton and at Oxford after."

He nodded. And he'd worked as diligently as ever for the rest of the afternoon, only to hear his tutor saying to his father as he made his way to the front door, "He is quite hopeless in his numbers. Beyond my ability to teach, I'm afraid."

Andrew knew his father might come in after, and so he'd raced through all the rooms at the back of the house and out the back door. He hadn't stopped running until he'd reached the Westchesters'. A pie sat in the window of their kitchen. The smell alone welcomed him with a feeling of relief. He burst through the front door just as Mrs. Westchester was rounding the stairs and stood there, his lips quivering.

"Oh come, child."

He hadn't been a child necessarily. It was high time for

him to grow up. But at the time, he'd felt in great need of the exact kind of love that Mrs. Westchester had offered, a warm enveloping hug and non-judgmental air.

Penny had come around the corner just then, and Mrs. Westchester had sat them both down with pie fresh from the kitchen, and taught him numbers herself.

Something about the way Mrs. Westchester explained things made much more sense to Andrew than what his tutor had been trying to say.

But no matter what he'd tried to explain to his father when they met later, Andrew was still sent to Eton the following semester.

And looking back, he knew it was for the best. If he'd known his parents would pass away as early as they had and that he'd be thrown into the role of estate owner, he would have been grateful to go. Though he missed his parents, he missed the Westchesters more.

Penny wrote him now and then. She told him of her own studies, of the trees and how much they'd grown, of her mother. She never mentioned her father. And Andrew was surprised to learn of his passing through mutual acquaintances at school.

When he returned home mid-term, he had started to see Penny in a new way. And she'd responded to his weak attempts at flirting.

Nothing happened between them, not a kiss certainly, but one afternoon, under their willow tree, the branches hiding them inside a lovely shade of green, he'd been carried away by emotion.

"Must you go back to school?" Penny's pout spoke for the both of them.

"I must. You know I must. But I will write. The terms go quickly, and I'll return."

"How do I know you won't forget me?" She'd stepped closer, looking with wide blue eyes up into his face.

At the time, he'd thought her the most beautiful person in the world and his best friend besides.

"I could never forget you. When I come back, I will prove just how much I…" He'd stammered a moment but when she stepped nearer, and her eyes shimmered with happiness, he continued, "I love you."

"Oh, I love you too. We shall make the best of things apart until we can be together again and never be parted." Her arms flung around him, and he hugged her back and at the moment, their plans had seemed perfectly reasonable to him.

But she'd not been as interested when he'd returned. Her response had been friendly but aloof, and he had drifted away from amorous feelings. His exit to London had been somewhat of a relief. He had assumed for her as well as for him.

Until she'd begun writing.

He couldn't make sense of it.

Was she mercenary? She'd never seemed to care one whit about his title or wealth before. But without their father all these years, perhaps things had fallen apart?

He made a note to ask his solicitor to investigate their financial dealings as much as could be known.

He continued with the letter, no longer reveling in the memories, more feeling entrapped by them.

Mrs. Westchester closed her portion of the letter, "You are as dear as any son to me. I long for the day you become my son, truly."

He groaned.

Penny's letter was full of descriptions of the local balls

and events. She was looking forward to the Maypole. She asked every few lines when he would return to experience it all with her. She mentioned a new family in the neighborhood, one with many brothers. It seemed to pop up out of nowhere, and he wondered about her intentions there. But then she moved on to the trees and toward the end, she said, *"The willow continues to grow. I long for the day we will once again meet there and you can make good on our promises. I've missed you. This time apart has allowed us to grow and become prepared for each other. But now all I want is for you to be back in my life. Come home when you can."*

He let the letter drop to his desk. How could she have returned to these old feelings? And her mother as well. And the intensity expressed just did not make sense. They'd not been that intense even when testing out a new direction between them. He'd made no promises. Surely she knew that. And she should not be writing him. Obviously she was trying to establish a level of intimacy that merited a union between them. It all felt very forced.

He ran a hand through his hair again and again, but no solutions came to mind.

Then a knock, followed by the abrupt entrance of Charity.

He jumped to his feet, sliding all sheets of the correspondence off his desk. "Miss Charity!"

His exasperated servant arrived behind her. "A Miss Charity to see you, my lord."

"Thank you, Hansen."

When the door had shut, Andrew shook his head. "You cannot simply come over to my house." He burned with embarrassment at what she might think of his bare home. He was certainly not making any great strides in impressing the woman.

"And why can't I? I'm here to visit your aunt, if you must know, and I thought I'd see how you were, locked in your study, while I was at it." She sat without being asked. "Besides, no one is going to think two bits of anything untoward about you and me. They'll all assume the obvious."

"Which is?"

"That I am here with some outlandish idea, and you are the only man fool enough to join me in my bluestocking ways."

"That's a sorry state for you and I." He rubbed his face.

"Are you well?"

With one eye, he peered at her from between his fingers.

"You are not well." She stood like she might approach. He shuffled the papers beneath his desk further.

"I am well, I'm fine." He cleared his throat. "I have received troubling news. And you are here in my home. Even if you refuse to see it, we're open to some bit of scandal." He moved around the desk. "But now that you're here…"

"Are you really that troubled that I have come?"

He thought of all the reasons he should be troubled, all the unfinished mess that the letters required, but when he opened his mouth to answer her, he could only respond to her radiant hope with something mild. "You are exactly correct. You could be here to visit my aunt. You are in the right of it. I needn't worry so much for your reputation." He strained against his cravat.

"No, you needn't. It has survived many a faux pas."

"But not the kinds of situations that might truly damage. You do need to be careful about those things, about men, going into seedy parts of London alone." He winced inside, hoping she would take his meaning well.

"And this visit is akin to going into the seedier parts of London alone?" Her eyebrow rose in challenge.

"Certainly not. I'm bringing it up in hopes that it too will be remembered."

She laughed. "I'm not one bit bothered, and besides, my sisters are coming to join us."

"They are?"

"Yes, we have come to help you decorate the place."

Nothing could have surprised him more.

"For you see, I'm not as uncouth and uneducated as you seem to believe. We all come at the invitation of your aunt."

He followed her out of the door thankfully and into a more appropriate part of the house, one where servants would join them. And perhaps his aunt if she'd truly invited them. "Why would she do such a thing?"

"She mentioned that you'd expressed a thought about decorating and that she was old enough to have done so ten times over. She thought that we might enjoy it more." Charity shrugged like this wasn't the oddest thing that had ever happened to the two of them. And they'd experienced odd things.

"I suppose." He indicated she precede him into the front parlor where his aunt was already seated.

She stood. "I'm so pleased you have come."

"Thank you for inviting me. My sisters will join us shortly."

"Excellent. I've asked the servants to bring in the swatches I have already, and we can of course get more. I will ask Francois Renault to join us."

"Francois Renault?" The name did not sound familiar.

"Yes, He's a wonderful decorator that will aid us in ordering the correct fabrics and finding furniture and fitting

71

rugs." She nodded decisively and patted a chair near her. "Please, come sit, Miss Charity. I will have a luncheon brought in when it's time. This will take a good many hours."

Andrew wasn't certain what to say. He sat beside Charity, uncomfortably on the edge of his seat.

She turned to him and her smile glowed with happiness, the kind that usually reassured whatever was amiss in his world, but those kinds of smiles would not reassure when he had another woman claiming an obligation from him.

The very presence of unfinished business of such a grave nature weighed on him. What was he to say? What should he do? How did one respectfully decline the existence of a romantic understanding?

The largest problem with his predicament being that he had become accustomed to approaching Charity with his life dilemmas, or at least, solving other people's injustices and problems. His natural inclination was to talk to her.

And yet, he couldn't.

How could he let her know Penny was pushing things this far? He couldn't. Not when he hoped to…

He couldn't finish the thought, not with her sitting beside him, not when she and her sisters had come to help decorate his home. He was already having the devil of a time holding his tongue where she was involved. And entangling what he would like to say with the guilt of his past would not help his case.

She placed a hand on his shoulder. "Are you certain you're well?" The care he saw in her eyes could well-nigh be his undoing.

He opened his mouth and then closed it.

Voices sounded in the hall and he stood, turning toward

the Standish sisters as they were announced. "Lady Morley, Lady Dennison, Mrs. Sullivan."

The three lowered in immaculate curtseys. And Andrew was reminded what he always thought when with them—the sisters had class.

He could only be grateful for the help of so many.

Charity hurried forward. "My sisters." They kissed cheeks and chattered away for what probably felt like the briefest of moments together, then turned as one to greet him: four beautiful ladies, with full smiles, excited to come and help him and his aunt.

"I don't know what to say." He bowed over each hand, placing a kiss, then straightened. "My aunt has us started."

Then Francois Renault was announced, and the room became a flutter of conversation and activity as samples were piled according to preference and paint and furniture were decided.

He quickly saw how little he was needed and left them to it.

Charity's soft smile as he stepped out of the room warmed him and gave him courage for what he must do.

Once in the quiet of his office, he took out a quill and ink, dipped and began to write. He thanked Mrs. Westchester for all her years of care, for the memories he carried and for the love she'd shared with him. He did not write Penny, but told her mother that he was happy for their correspondence because it brought back the feelings of youth.

One section he toiled over, unsure how to phrase his words precisely. *"While I will always hold these memories dear, my affections in regards to anything other than brotherly affection toward Penny have ceased. I naturally wish you both the best. When Penny comes for a Season, I would be more than happy to remake the acquaintance, but as far as an inquiry as to my intentions, Penny moved on years ago, and I have followed her example, so much so, that I have none of an amorous nature.*

Consider yourself free of any entanglements with me."

He breathed out in relief as he signed the letter, sealed it and then rang for his servant.

When the footman appeared at the doorway, Charity peeked in from behind him.

He laughed at her persistence, stood, and handed the letter to his servant. "Please send this express as soon as you can."

The man bowed and left him and Charity in a partially opened doorway.

"This is quite a coup you have organized in my home. I'm feeling quite taken over."

"It cannot be too disturbing a feeling as your home will be ready for guests when we are through."

"Am I in need of guests?"

"Certainly, if you wish to begin entertaining." She smiled and put her hand on his arm. "Come. We wish to show you what we'd decided."

"Have decisions been made then?"

"They have, and I believe Mr. Francois Renault is the most excited."

He laughed. "But you approve?" He paused, watching her face. "Are the changes precisely to your liking?"

A slight pink colored her cheeks. "They are indeed. You have a lovely home here."

He nodded. "Then I shall be all the more pleased." He cleared his throat. "In fact, I should like all improvements to be approved by you." He flicked a gaze in her direction but then kept his face forward.

"Oh, I'm the least expert. For that reason, I petitioned my sisters to aid us. For I should be thinking more of the library and they the drapes."

It was not for her particular expertise in décor that he most especially wished for her opinions, of course, but now did not seem the time to more clearly state his wishes. Nor was he certain how she would respond.

When he entered the room, they had everything out on the floor in front of him: fabric samples, pictures from papers, drawings; he was quite impressed. "Well, this is something. You shall save my dear aunt and myself from the dullness we live in."

"Won't this be lovely, Wilfred?" Aunt Victoria's smile and obvious enjoyment beamed across the room.

Charity put a hand over her mouth, trying to hide her amusement. Should he tell her that except for very few people, his closest friends called him Andrew? Watching her struggle and obviously enjoying herself immensely, he decided to wait.

CHAPTER 7

*A*s soon as Charity stepped back in the door of the duchess' townhome, a maid approached and curtseyed. "His Grace sent me looking for you. He'd like to see you in his study."

"Thank you." Charity smiled. The summons was odd, but the happiness of being such a help to Lord Lockhart and of seeing her sisters, of discussing the plans for the school, all of the wonderful lingering feelings carried her to the door with a happy expectation that the morning could only bring more of the same.

She knocked.

"Enter."

She pushed open a surprisingly heavy door. She'd never been in his study.

The duchess sat in a chair near the fire. The walls were lined with books. One large portrait of a man who might have been His Grace's father hung high on the wall behind his desk, and the duke himself sat behind the dark wood top. It was obvious that a conversation of some sort had been midstride before Charity entered. But the duchess' face was a well-trained blank, so Charity received no clues from her.

"Ah, Miss Charity. Come in. Sit with us."

A good sign. He seemed in a pleasant enough mood.

"Thank you."

"You were just visiting Lady Hackney?"

"Yes, my sisters and I. She and Lord Lockhart were in desperate need. Their home is but a bare place of walls and some furniture. I'm happy she invited us."

Their responding smiles were placid. The duke pressed his fingers together. "And what are his intentions toward you?"

Charity was taken aback for a moment. She swallowed twice and tried to keep her face as emotionless as the duchess'. "I...I am unsure at the moment."

"And how long have you been...friends?" The duke's eyes were kind. He was trying to help her in some way which was completely unclear at the moment.

"This is our second Season. He comes to our salons, is a large help there and a good influence."

"Yes." The duke shifted some papers around on his desk. "There have been others who have inquired after you."

"Inquired?" Who would have? The women in her meetings? Other men? She raised a hand to her mouth.

"I have been personally approached by quite a few and others have been pointed out to me. It seems you have a long list of admirers."

The air felt tight around her, and she wished above all things to leave that room for a moment. She'd not considered the role the duke would play in her Season when she'd agreed to come. In truth, she'd not considered that she'd have any suitors. "I don't know what to say."

"This is certainly good news. Lord Granville is highly

interested, and my wife said you two have an excellent rapport."

"Oh yes, I enjoy him." She clenched her hands together.

"Lords Timmons, Sterling, and Kenworthy have expressed an interest. As well as one other that has shocked me, but the duchess seems to have been expecting it."

"Oh?" Charity looked from one to the other.

The duchess' mouth twitched, but that was all she would reveal.

"Lord Wessex."

Charity shook her head. "He cannot be serious."

"That's precisely what I told my wife, but she assures me he is."

Charity heartfully disagreed but kept quiet for the moment, wondering how this would play out.

"I'm quite pleased. The Season has not even begun in full force, and we might be finished with it."

Her Grace cleared her throat.

"But I have been informed that we are in a good position and need to wait, because these sorts of declarations do not always come to fruition, and because I assume she is having a more enjoyable time than I watching your success." He turned to her and waited.

"Oh, well."

"If one of these men were to mean something to you already, then now is the best time to express your wishes."

She started to shake her head.

"Surely there has not been enough time to know." Her Grace's poised response was something to envy.

"If we were to encourage one or two of them, with vague and mild pleasantries...perhaps Lord Granville and Lord Sterling might be valuable options?" His Grace nodded encouragingly.

"Perhaps encouragement is too strong a word." Charity desperately thought of how best to proceed.

"But perhaps a dinner party where they were included might be just the thing." The duchess smiled.

Charity nodded. "Yes, that would be excellent." She twisted her hands in her lap. "If a man wishes to court me, this is the manner in which it happens?"

"Yes, if a man is courting you outside these official means, then it is highly suspect." The duke's longer than usual gaze struck her.

"And Lord Lockhart?" She wanted to bite back the words as soon as they left her mouth, not wishing to give away too much. But had he said anything? Did he think of her in that way?

"He has said nothing." The duke collected his papers into one pile.

She knew her mouth tugged down. But what could she do with that sort of disappointment?

The duchess stood and moved to Charity's side. "I cannot think he does not care."

The duke snapped his drawer shut. "But an honorable man would declare himself if he did, or stop giving the impression that he is about to. You must be free to make your way through the Season, to find a suitable match. He is by far the wealthiest man of our acquaintance, seems a good enough sort, except for his bluestocking ways, but you like that sort of thing. I do not know what holds him back, but it is a question to consider." He stood as well. "My wife has told me not to intervene as yet. I could ask him his intentions, but she has bid me wait."

Her Grace nodded, resting a hand on Charity's arm. "Give the man an opportunity to declare himself. Some men are timid about these things. And our Charity, she is not one for the faint of heart."

"Precisely my point there. But we shall let it ride its course a short time longer. In the meantime, I will move forward as directed. And you." He pointed a friendly finger in her direction. "Would do well to begin an active campaign to show attention to those who might interest you and discourage those who do not. Starting tonight."

"Tonight?"

"Yes, His Grace is taking us to Almack's."

Charity nodded, unsure how to feel about all the information she'd just realized in one conversation. Did Lord Lockhart view her on amiable terms only? Were they partners in an effort to change England and nothing more? His actions toward her were more than amiable. She thought she could tell. She assumed today that his response to her decorating the house had been very positive, intimate almost.

She frowned. But he'd left for most of the time and perhaps was only humoring their work. His aunt had planned the whole thing after all. Her heart clenched tighter. When she met the duke's eyes, she was surprised by a touch of compassion there.

"You will find a man who will take care of you and your children."

"And one that makes you happy." The duchess' hand on her arm was soft yet surprisingly strong. "Mark my words."

Charity's gratitude for the both of them grew. She'd come, using their hospitality to further her work, arrogantly thinking they would be but pawns to her plan. She now saw just how much she was in need of their wisdom and direction. "Thank you both."

"Of course, dear. We want the best for you."

Charity nodded. "I see that."

She was hurried off to her room where Lily waited with hot curling pins and one of Charity's best gowns laid out on the bed. "I guess we are off to Almack's this evening."

"Yes, miss. And happy I am to see you sooner rather than later if we're going to get you ready."

Charity spent the whole of their preparations saying little. Her mind raced through most of her memories of Lord Lockhart. Then she tried to focus on her specific duties to help get the school off the ground, and her mind immediately went back to Lord Lockhart. She tried to think of the words to her favorite Treatise on Women and Lockhart's voice, quoting it, came to mind. She even attempted to remember times with her sisters, before Lockhart existed in her life, and still, he intruded.

His smile, his eyes lighting up when he saw her, surely these were signs that he cared. All the time he spent with her, at her meetings, his urgency in assisting in her causes…Was all of this merely a shared interest? A true devotion to change? And nothing more?

She almost slouched in a heap at the thought, but that would have disturbed the careful curls that Lily was creating around her face.

He had not wanted to dance with her the last time they were together. He'd not ever shown the slightest inclination to court her, only spend time with her, but nothing that typically indicated courting. Perhaps he was trying to send her a message she had doggedly refused to see?

She had to know.

She must find out.

All manner of plans circulated in her mind as to how a person would find out the nature of a man's affection. Her eyes flit to Lily. "Have you had a beau?"

She nearly dropped the pins in shock, and then her face colored. "Why, miss. I don't know if I should be talking about such things."

"I don't see why not. Have you?"

"A few." Her blush grew. "But nothing that was ever going to become something serious."

"How do you know?"

She waved her hand around. "Oh, they just don't see me that way."

"How do you know that?"

Lily paused. Their eyes met in the mirror. "Are you wondering how I know if a man is interested in me?"

"That's exactly what I'm wondering."

"Well, now this might not work in the same manner for you as it does for me, but I always know when he kisses me."

Charity gasped. "How many men have you kissed?"

She clucked. "Now this is all part of the conversation I don't think I should be having with you, miss."

Charity stared her down and did not let up.

"Oh bother. What can I say? I've kissed quite a few, more than those three beaux I was talking about."

Charity stared at her with new eyes.

"Don't be looking at me like that, beggin' your pardon, miss, not when you needled the information out of me."

"Fair." Charity shook her head. "How many men have you kissed?"

"A good amount like I said, and forgive me, but your

sister would not be forgiving me for telling you anything more than that."

"And tell me again how you know a man is interested. If you kissed so many, do you mean to tell me every one of those men was interested?"

"Oh, certainly not." She clucked as if this were nothing, while Charity's whole world was rolling around on a ball, ready to wobble to its side. She'd never known a single other person who professed to kiss men like Lily had. She pinned another strand of hair. "You don't know they're interested simply *because* they kiss you. There are many men who will kiss you no matter how they feel about you. And most of them don't want to do anything more with you than that. But you know they are truly growing attached by the *manner* in which they kiss."

Charity couldn't have looked away from her maid's face if she tried. When she said no more, Charity prompted, "And?"

"Goodness, miss, you're like to get me fired."

"Unlikely since I'm your employer."

She eyed her a moment and then sighed. "This just isn't done, these kinds of conversations. I know you're more liberally minded than most, and I appreciate our banter, the manner in which we can be open, but you do know this is highly improper.'

"And I also know that you have information I want."

They stared each other down for the count of ten and then Lily laughed. "I couldn't keep it from you, not with you as persistent as you are."

"Precisely, now let us have the information."

"When he kisses you, you will know. He will be speaking his feelings to you through his kiss. It doesn't matter how long or short, you will know. Any other kiss might feel wonderful.

It might dazzle and amaze, but if he doesn't care, it won't have the same effect. You will know."

Charity was somewhat disappointed. Telling her she *would* know but not *how* she would know felt like no help at all. She frowned. "Since I've kissed no man and will have nothing to compare the experience, I find your input less than helpful."

"You will know. A woman knows in her core when a man's kiss is something special." She nodded with so much surety, Charity had half a mind to believe her.

Lily adjusted several pins, applied more rouge and then smiled. "You are finished, and might I say, I've never seen you look lovelier. And that's saying something."

"Thank you." With a mind full of kissing and Lord Lockhart and the many lords that His Grace wished her to know, Charity stood, slipped a reticule and fan over her wrist and stepped out the door, making wild attempts to school her expression and keep the blush from her face.

For the second time that Season, was she to attend a ball with simply the hope that she would converse with men? No ulterior motives in mind? No agenda?

She most certainly was, and she hardly knew herself.

But how could she know herself when she was suddenly so enamored with one man, one life outside her own. The day started and ended with thoughts of Lord Lockhart, and went from thinking him equally drawn to her and then only passably interested all in the same day, rotating between the two in such a wagon ride of bumps of emotion that she didn't know what more to do with herself on the subject. The duke's advice seemed more appropriate now than ever for her, for if she couldn't have Lord Lockhart, she would need *someone*.

Somehow, this hole in her heart would have to be filled, lest she be miserable all her days.

When she descended the stairs, the duke's expression of approval was surprisingly gratifying. Where she'd only previously viewed her appearance as a paltry substitute for the benefits of her mind and what she could do in the world, she now considered that it too might be something of value.

"You look well, my dear." Her Grace patted her cheek.

"Thank you."

The duke offered his arms to them both, and Charity felt precious indeed as she was escorted to the carriage and helped up inside. Two activities that had happened again and again, actions she often felt were a useless extra step to simply loading a carriage, now felt to be a powerful expression of caring.

They arrived at Almack's to the concluding advice from Her Grace along with a list of lords whom the duke wished for her to know better.

Charity's head spun. She had thought organizing baskets for the poor was a lot of work. This dizzying amount of information to remember compared in every way to those such activities.

As they were about to enter, the duchess whispered close. "Consider that who you marry opens doors of influence."

And with those words, Charity recognized just how important marrying well might be for her future ability to make a difference forever. Those words, combined with all previous conversation, motivated Charity to commit to take greater care of her own future marriage.

And with that thought, she determined to discover just how interested Lord Lockhart was in her, no matter what means became necessary.

CHAPTER 8

*L*ord Lockhart stepped into an overly large crush at Almack's. Why had he decided to come? What motivated this move into a previously unplanned activity? Going somewhere tonight when he'd been looking forward to a book by the fire?

A note from the Duchess of York with three words written on it. "Come to Almack's."

And so here he was.

Charity.

Confused as to why the note had come from the duchess, he stepped into the assembly room. People crowded in closer on all sides. How did people expect to converse at all in such a crush? They didn't quite jostle him. Such a thing as jostling seemed beneath them all, but they had precious little space in between them, and he wanted nothing more than to stretch his arms up and all around him. Confound them, why again must they attend Almack's? He looked for Charity. Perhaps he could convince her that a walk outside would be just the thing.

A cluster of men in the corner made him laugh. He'd found her. If she was in high form on one of her crusades, perhaps his evening wouldn't be a wash after all. He'd listen for the subject and join her. Between the two of them, they could spread the word.

He still hadn't seen her, but as he got closer, her laugh rang out, and he stepped nearer. The group laughed uproariously. And then Lord Kenworthy tilted his head forward, and Andrew caught sight of Charity.

Her cheeks aglow, her eyes on fire, her mouth opened and free in a lovely easy smile. And everyone around her was captivated.

Including Andrew.

His feet would not move. His thoughts stopped. And his tongue went so dry he didn't think he'd ever use it again. Who was this Athena? She was easily the most beautiful woman in the room, the most beautiful he'd ever seen. He was equal parts completely beguiled by her and wishing for his cloak to lay across her shoulders.

Lord Wessex leaned closer to her, whispering something in her ear that brought a brighter pink to her cheeks. The others said something to razz her.

Andrew stepped closer.

Her mellow voice reached him, sending bolts of something partly pleasant partly uncomfortable down to his feet.

"Oh, Lord Wessex. You are just toying with me. We all know it." She swatted at him with her fan.

"Tell us your latest thoughts on Napoleon," Lord Kenworthy called out.

Andrew bristled. Was he making fun of her? But as he looked closer, he thought not. The men were fascinated with Charity.

Had they all suddenly grown some sense and appreciated all the wonderful things about her? His heart sank. His hopes to be with Charity were in serious jeopardy.

But he stood taller, undeterred and pushed his way through so that he was standing at her front. "Miss Charity." He held out his hand.

"Lord Lockhart. It's good to see you." Her face lit with more happiness which gratified him to no end.

"I've come for our set?"

The men all around her laughed.

And Charity's shone with amusement but also a touch of disappointment. "I'm sorry, they're all taken."

His mouth dropped open. They'd always had the first set. They used the time to plan strategies for the ball. Well, except for last time they were at a ball together. He'd stayed as far away as possible. The men were watching him. He'd been quiet too long.

He bowed. "I'll leave you to it then." He turned.

As he walked away, someone said something about Lord Lockhart losing his place if he wasn't careful. And the others laughed.

He made his way to the exit. He had no need to stick around.

But the Duchess of York stepped in his path. "Where are you going?"

"Leaving. Every dance is taken."

"And so you will give her up? Just like that?"

"What do you want me to do, create a scene? Force my way in?"

She clucked. "Don't be a sore loser. Wait for her. Be here. She'll come to you when she wants a break. She'll find you, and you will know that she is still interested."

"Is she?"

"I'd imagine so. She's only been here at this ball for thirty minutes. Do you suppose her allegiance would change in so short a time?"

"Does she have an allegiance?" His mouth tugged, ready to show his hope rising.

"You'll have to discover that for yourself." She turned from him.

And he decided to stay.

Lord Wessex led Charity out onto the floor. And that was enough to make Andrew wish to stalk off again. But he kept his hessians firmly planted on the floor. He would stick it out. A devilish idea caught him. He moved to the edge of the dance floor, crossed his arms, and watched.

With a man like Lord Wessex, they couldn't be too careful. He could kick himself for not declaring his intentions sooner. His eyes sought the Duke of York—who was watching him to his surprise. His Grace's eyebrows went up.

Andrew nodded. He would speak to the man straight away.

Between them was a whole ballroom full of people—including those dancing what promised to be the longest country dance of all time.

As his gaze followed her down the line, laughing and moving each step as though lifted by joy itself, he was astounded that he'd not seen this side of Charity yet before. Certainly, she was always full of energy. She was always about the importance of doing things. And he knew she received great satisfaction from her usual activities, but fun? He realized this was one of the first moments he was witness to Charity having fun just for the sake of it.

And he vowed to offer her this part of her life more often.

When their gazes met, hers held questions, but he just nodded.

Lord Wessex smirked at him and let his hands linger longer in their dance.

When he led Charity off the floor, another lord escorted her right back out.

Andrew stood his ground.

From the side of the floor, he watched as Charity danced set after set with all manner of men laughing and flattering her, bringing that smile to her face, the one that showed her fun side. The one he wanted to see more of, directed at him.

At last, while the orchestra was taking a break, she wandered over to him. He lifted her hand to his mouth immediately. "You shine. As if the candles all turned their glow to you." He meant every word, but judging by her reaction, he perhaps should have considered the timing of such a declaration.

Her eyes narrowed. "Are you making fun of me?"

"What? No."

"The candles turned their glow on me?" Her one eyebrow rose so high he wished to retract every word.

"No, really, Miss Charity. I don't say things like that enough...ever...but the words came unsolicited from my lips. Perhaps I'm not as well-spoken as some." The pause that followed, accentuated by his own pleading expression, must have softened her.

"Well, that's great then. Thank you." She stood close. Probably as close as they always stood, but tonight he was aware of every shift of her skirts, of the air between them that he wished to shrink, or his hands that hung awkwardly at his sides when he wished they were pulling her closer, or at minimum, holding her hand in his.

He realized too much time had passed since he'd said anything. These kinds of silences never happened between them before.

They both began at the same time. He again wished to take back his words. "What are we working on tonight?"

Because she said, "You look handsome. I like the more colorful jackets on you."

So he added, "You are beautiful."

They were silent for a breath before she murmured, "Thank you."

The strings started up again, and he knew his time was short. But every thought of what to say left.

Lord Granville approached with a bow and then she was back on the floor, one man after another until the second to last set.

And then the duchess approached. "Her last set had to leave early." The words fell around him as she walked by, and he wasted no time on the heels of the man who was about to tell her he was leaving before their set.

As the words left the man's mouth, Andrew held out his hand.

She hardly had a moment to respond to her first partner before Andrew was leading her out on the floor.

The familiar three-step rhythm of the waltz sounded. "And now I am to be rewarded for an agony of an evening."

She laughed. "An agony? I've had a delightful time. Did you know that Lord Kenworthy's estate boasts an orange orchard in a green house? That must be a delicious green house. Can you imagine the scents." Her face lifted in ecstasy at the thought, and Andrew immediately made plans to order a greenhouse and orange orchard be built and cultivated on his estate.

"I've been in agony watching you in the arms of so many when my own arms ached for this moment." He was bold. But apparently it was time to be bold.

Instead of responding with pleasure or a blush or a laugh or even sarcastically making fun, she seemed to bristle in his arms. And she looked away.

"What did I say?"

"What are you after, Lord Lockhart?"

"After?"

"Yes."

Thoughts of the Duke of York, waiting for him across the ballroom tugged at guilty strings. "Perhaps I should pay a visit to the Duke of York?"

Her eyes lit with surprise. And then a small smile tugged at her lips, beautiful full lips that begged for attention all of a sudden. "I know he is making himself available for just such a visit."

"Is he?"

She nodded.

And he sensed the urgency. How many other men had already approached him? He realized the problem with his neglect. He'd come across as a complete cad. Dash his hesitancy. He should have made his intentions known, early and often.

"I must hold my tongue until then. I realize I've neglected to move forward as you deserve. And now knowing that you could choose any man here, I only pray I'm not too late."

She stepped closer, her face, inches from his, her hands resting on his arm and shoulder, and then her gaze went to his lips causing an intense burning to begin under her gaze, a warmth that spread to his chest. He wanted only to pull her close up against him, to wrap her in his arms forever as his lips covered hers.

She stood taller.

He forgot everything, her full mouth parting. Their breath mingled before someone coughed. And she jerked away.

He blinked twice and then cleared his head. *Daft.* "Apologies."

She refused to look at him.

The Duke of York certainly was though.

He dipped his head.

The final chords played. He couldn't let her go, not yet. "Miss Charity. Might I come tomorrow?"

"Yes." She lifted her lashes and smiled. And he knew everything would be all right. He would come as early as possible, meet with the duke, ask permission to court her, and then he would be free to declare himself.

"I shall come at my earliest possible convenience."

"I'd like that." She turned away. Her hand was on his arm, but she seemed to wish to leave his presence as soon as possible.

He walked with her to the duke and duchess, one looking overly pleased and the other overly irritated.

Andrew cleared his throat. "Might I have a moment with you tomorrow morning?"

"I think you'd better."

"Yes, very good, Your Grace." Andrew bowed and then made his way out of the assembly room.

As his carriage approached the townhome he shared with his aunt, an unusual amount of lights flickered from inside their front parlor. Was his aunt still up? His feet were light as he stepped down from the carriage and leapt up to the front door.

Even though the whole of that evening was spent out of Charity's company, even though he'd bungled their dance, almost kissed her in front of everyone, and their final conversation had been as awkward as any they'd had, Andrew could only feel pleased. He was at last going to declare himself to the duke. He would stare into her beautiful eyes and tell her what he'd been aching to say, that he loved her.

He loved Charity.

His whistle came unbidden as he stepped into his front entry hall but stopped dead in his throat at one voice he never could have expected.

"Miss Penny?"

Three ladies stood as he entered the room. His aunt, Mrs. Westchester and Miss Penny. They curtseyed together, and he responded with a bow. His dear aunt looked as though she'd fall over in exhaustion. The other two seemed perhaps travel-worn but otherwise awake. Miss Penny's face had gone a bit white, but he imagined that might have been nerves.

Mrs. Westchester stepped forward, her arms out. "Come here, son." The kindly face that welcomed him was the same face that had wiped scrapes, had soothed loneliness, had listened to him speak of plans for the future.

He instinctively moved toward her. As shocking as this visit was and portended nothing good for him, a wave of nostalgia, a wave of longing for a mother figure in his life, filled him, and he wrapped her in the hug of his youth. "It's good to see you, Mrs. Westchester."

"You too, my dear." She patted him. She smelled the same, a mixture of cooking spices and vanilla. And her embrace felt the same, though perhaps a bit more wiry. As he stepped away, she turned. "Miss Penny and I have arrived this evening, and we know it isn't done, but we are practically family so we have waited here for your return, not wanting to miss a moment."

His aunt's face was a blank. She likely wished them gone.

He was aghast at their treatment of her but vowed to make it up to her as soon as they left.

He turned at last to Miss Penny. She looked...older. She'd matured into a well-looking debutante. He was certain she'd be much sought after. He wished her success. But he felt none of the old familiarity. She seemed a stranger to him.

After the sparkle of Charity, this new Miss Penny seemed subdued, as if the light had been squelched. "Miss Penny."

"Oh, Andrew. It's been too long."

He bowed over her hand, sticking with formality while he attempted to clear his head.

They sat, she on a sofa, he on a chair. He crossed a leg over his knee. "You look well." He smiled.

Great relief filled her expression. "Thank you."

"You both seem to be in good health? How is the neighborhood?"

"Everyone is just wonderful. You are spoken of often. Your tenants are in excellent stead. And as I'm certain your steward reports, the estate is thriving."

"Yes, I feel fortunate indeed in the turn of events in my favor."

"I always knew that lone boy we took in under our wings would come to make something remarkable of himself."

"I don't know how much influence I actually had over things. Inheritances come quite without talent."

"Oh tosh. It is certainly your ingenuity that has the tenants learning new skills and new methods. They are the most vibrant and happiest in the valley."

A great sense of satisfaction filled him. "I'm happy to hear it. For I take great responsibility thinking of them in my care."

They talked for a moment more, and after two yawns from his aunt and the fatigue weighing down his thoughts, he cleared his throat. "I do appreciate you coming straight away to see me, but there is time left in the Season, surely. We must retire and spare my aunt."

"Oh, forgive us." Mrs. Westchester looked supremely uncomfortable as she shifted in her seat. "There is a rather urgent reason for coming and for waiting. We couldn't spare another second before we imparted news of the gravest kind."

He leaned forward, his mind listing all the possibilities.

"Perhaps I might speak with you alone?" Mrs. Westchester indicated the doorway.

"I do believe I shall retire at any rate." Aunt stood.

They bid her farewell properly and then as they returned to their seats, Mrs. Westchester brought a handkerchief to her nose. Before he knew what else was happening, her shoulders were shaking with her sorrow.

Miss Penny stared at the floor.

Andrew was torn between keeping his seat and jumping to comfort the woman. "My dear Mrs. Westchester. What can be done?"

She waved him away. "I will regain my composure. I must." She breathed deeply, with a hand to her chest, blinking back tears. And then nodded. "There. You see."

Miss Penny still had not looked anywhere but at the floor since this new outburst of emotion.

"There is nothing for it but to say, Andrew, our dear Andrew, we have come to beg your assistance. You might be the only person we trust, as it is the family kind of situation certainly."

"What is it? I shall attempt with all my power to assist in whatever way I may."

Mother and daughter exchanged looks, and a certain uneasiness overtook him. But he waited, growing more uncomfortable as a silence continued.

At last, Mrs. Westchester shook her head. "There is nothing for it but to simply state the facts as they stand. "Our Miss Penny is with child."

He gripped the side of his chair with a sudden panic.

"She has been taken advantage of in a most ruthless manner and then cast aside."

Penny would not meet his gaze.

"You very well know that there is nothing for it but to marry in haste or to live out her days in shame."

He shook his head. "Certainly, there are more options."

But she had not stopped talking and he couldn't tell if she heard him at all.

"She is of course most suited to a dear friend, someone who's known her the whole of her life, who would not hold this over her head the rest of her life. And since you have spent the first part of this Season without forming a formal attachment, I wonder if perhaps we might meet both needs right here. Bring two best friends back together, and save our dear Penny from a fate worse than death."

They both turned to him, Penny at last meeting his gaze. And when he said nothing for what must have been deemed too great a length of time, Mrs. Westchester cleared her throat. "And when you already have an understanding between you…"

He shook his head. "Surely you received my express."

"That does not signify."

"What do you mean?"

"Changing one's mind is not a valid reason to break off an engagement. Particularly if a child is involved."

He jerked to his feet. "Surely you don't mean to insinuate...You know that I have had nothing...I will not sit here and listen to this falsehood."

"No matter." Mrs. Westchester rose. "We think of you as family. If you do your duty by her, marry her straight away, nothing more needs to be said about it."

"And what if I told you that I have made connections, that I am on my way tomorrow to speak to a woman's sponsor?"

Her expression was so smug, he wished to wipe it from her face. She nearly purred her response. "Then I know that you are unattached as of right now, and therefore free to honor your prior engagement."

"There was no prior engagement."

"We say there was."

Penny was once again looking down at her slippers.

"Might I have a word with Miss Penny?"

"Of course." She slipped out and shut the door.

In two large strides, he then opened it again. "Timothy would you please join us?"

"Yes, my lord." His loyal servant stepped just inside the door.

He lifted Penny's hand in his own and waited until she looked up into his face. The hesitancy there, the shame, softened his heart toward her. But not enough to let her see his softening.

"I loved him," she whispered. "Mama doesn't want you to know. He didn't force himself."

"Who is he?"

"A tenant farmer."

"Mine?"

She nodded. Then she reached a hand out, clutching his arm in a most desperate manner. "If I don't wed a man in the next month, all will be known. I shall be shamed forever. And my life ruined, as well as my child's life."

The truth of her words barreled into him.

"You are our only hope. Who else do we know that would step in? Who else has such a strong tie? Who else has Mother cared for?"

Her implication hit him where it was supposed to. Right in the gut. And he'd already been feeling nudges of responsibility where she was concerned. Writing that letter telling her he no longer had feelings was freeing as much as it was a force of willpower, but now this, this desperate need from a family who had been everything to him growing up, lowered on him like an anvil. His breathing tightened. Was this his future? Was he to marry a woman who pined for another? While he longed for Charity with his every breath?

He swallowed twice. "This is news indeed. I shall need some time. It's late. I think you should leave."

Her face went white. "You won't deny me!" She threw herself into his arms. "You cannot deny me. You mustn't. I will be ruined! My mother, my child." Her desperate eyes peered up into his face. "Would you have all that on your hands? Would you be able to be happy with someone else, knowing that peace came at the cost of lives destroyed?"

An odd assortment of their shared past flashed before his eyes. Games on the green fields that separated their estates; dinners with their families; all the moments he was joining in whatever she was doing, instead of at his home. All the times he himself had been lonely and desperate in a world that seemed to have abandoned him, and she had rescued him.

"Just go."

Her stricken face would haunt him. But she nodded and turned from him. "We'll leave our direction with your servant."

He didn't answer, his eyes unseeing, his heart in a turmoil, his mind drifting back to a past ripe with sorrow and loss.

CHAPTER 9

*E*arly the next morning, far earlier than was polite, Andrew stood at the front door to the Duke of York's townhome. The butler eyed him for a moment and then let him enter, turning in the entryway. "Wait here, please."

What would he say? He didn't know. He hoped the Duke could shed some light on his situation. How would he explain things to Charity? Would she think him a cad for ignoring the girl? Would she think him a cad for aiding the girl? Somehow, no matter what he would have to do, moving forward, he wanted her to think well of him. "I want to do the right thing." His mutterings were louder than he expected, but no one seemed to have heard.

After a moment, the butler returned. "She is waiting for you in the kitchen."

He started. He hadn't specified. So of course the servant would think he was there to see Charity. But instead of correcting him, Andrew decided to go see her, a sort of painful torture, while he waited for her father to be free. He nodded and made his way straight there. Was it odd that he knew the direction to most rooms in the house? The kitchen even? No matter. She was likely putting together something for the school. He'd be much relieved to be involved in a work, anything, using his hands.

But she sat in a corner while the kitchen staff were busy making what smelled to be a delicious breakfast. She had a cup in her hands, and she seemed lost in thought. Her hair was disheveled, her marvelous curls cascading all around her, tied back in a bit of a ribbon that was no match for their power. Her nose was lifted, her brow serene, and as she closed her eyes to some delicious thought, he was frozen in his tracks. He loved this woman. He loved her so fiercely he didn't know what to do with himself. Only an extreme force of will kept him from throwing himself at her feet and begging to be married, right then.

She turned to him, her eyes opening. And somehow the reality of her awareness calmed his raptures somewhat. But then her face lit in a joyful smile.

And he was once again battling the desire to throw himself at her feet. Was he not here to talk to the duke about courting and then marrying her? Could he not move forward with the long-held desire of his heart? Could he ignore the pleadings of a longtime friend?

She patted the seat beside her. "I was just thinking of you."

As he joined her, he scooped her hand up in his. "I am always thinking of you." He placed his lips on her bare knuckles with the hunger of one who knew he might never get to do so again. She might never know that the feel of her skin on his lips was seared there in memory.

"Have I ever told you how much I like your hands?" She

surprised him by taking his in her own smaller ones and with cool fingers, traced the lines in his palm.

"You have never, no." His voice sounded far away to his ears. Everything seemed far away except for her head, bowed over his hand, and her fingers sending fiery sensations through him. Did she realize that with every touch she was sealing him hers?

She continued, seemingly unaware of his emotional upheaval. "Yes, they're strong. I've seen them do great work. But they're soft. I'd like to hold them, just like this, in front of the fire." She lifted her lashes. The love that shone back stole his breath. All ability to do any duty toward Penny swept away in the gale force of her love shining at him full in the face. "And so you shall." He reached out his other hand and ran a finger down the side of her face. "You are beautiful."

Her laugh sounded like music. "Even like this? In such a state? The duchess would be horrified."

"Especially like this." He toyed with one of her curls. "You are magnificent, like those brilliant orators, stirring people's hearts to greatness, that's you. Just the sight of you does that for me."

Her eyes shone. And then she lifted his hand, turned it over, and brought it up to her lips. Their softness caressed his rough knuckle, turning it into something gallant, for her, he would be anything, do anything.

His eyes could not look away as her lips parted and placed the tiniest bit of moisture on his skin. Their softness calling to him, he then closed his eyes against the urge to pull her up from her seat and into his arms. "You will be the death of me, woman."

Her laugh filled the kitchen. "The death of you? What will it be death by?"

"Pistols at dawn."

"Heavens, such a violent one. I had thought more like poison by mushroom."

He laughed at her ridiculousness but then shook his head, gravely. "Pistols it is. When the duke finds out I've thoroughly and completely ruined his guest by placing a much longed for kiss on her beautiful mouth."

Her mouth dropped open, and for a moment she said nothing.

Had he at last found a speechless Charity?

Was his kiss welcome? He searched her face and could find no evidence of any emotion. Besides shock. That didn't bode well; perhaps he was too bold. But there it stood. He would not take back his words. He would not pander about in an effort to lighten their intensity. He was of a mind to make good on his promise and kiss her senseless if she'd let him.

Was he desperate? Was he trying to do anything in his power to seal her as his and wipe away any obligation for another? Or did he simply love her so much it hurt? Both. Surely more love than desperation.

She stood, her eyes filled with longing and she tugged at his hand, pulling him to his feet—in complete obedience to her every command.

As soon as he straightened, she was in his arms, her hands climbing up his chest, her feet up on her toes. And her mouth over his.

He responded immediately as their softness sent a shiver through him. His arms encircled her and his hands stretched out over her back, pulling her as close as was possible to him. Charity. His Charity. His mouth moved over hers, seeking, exploring, glorying in the exhilaration of holding such a woman. She smiled beneath him, and he kissed her lips back into their task of accepting his love, his desire, his promise to be hers forever. Forever. He consumed her mouth in a desperate frenzy, fighting against the sense of something intruding, something disrupting. *No.* He would let nothing stand in their way. Not even Penny.

And then the image of Penny entered his mind. A shattering tear ripped through the center of him. Her eyes, her plea, the desperation in her life. And he buckled over in pain.

"What? What is it?" Charity's arms were around him, helping lower him to his chair. "Bring some tea." Her shout and the sounds of the staff rushing about seemed as though miles from him. Her voice in his ear, her kisses on his head while he hid from her, his face in his hands. The torture of his situation stealing even his well-being. With shaking hands, he clutched at her. He could only guess what horrors were written on his face. She gasped upon seeing him.

His voice, sounding raspy, left his lips unsolicited, spoke the words that honor dictated. "I have never been more true than I have right now. Remember. No matter what happens, this is how I feel. This is what I want. I'm not free to do this right now." Then he stood. "I fear I shall die every day for the rest of my life."

Then he left the kitchen.

Surely she called after him. Or maybe she did not. He didn't know the effect his words had, he had not met her eyes when he cowardly ran, and now he may never know.

He hurried through their home, trying to leave as soon as possible, hoping to avoid contact with the duke, running from his happiness, from his sanity, running from the greatest desire of his heart and running from his shame. To create in Charity such a passion, such a love. Her kiss astounded him. She was full of fire, full of all the energy she usually exerted toward anything, and that strength had been focused on him for one blessed moment. He'd likely never be the same.

But to experience that passion and then dash it to pieces in her face, was the most cad-like thing he'd ever done. And he'd never be able to look her in the face again.

"Wilfred!" He would have laughed at her use of his seldom-used name if the situation wasn't what it was.

"Stop right there!" Her command did not allow disobeying.

His feet jerked him to a stop. But he reached a hand out to the wall to steady himself.

"What do you think you're doing?" Her voice was loud. Too loud. Soon all in the house would be apprised.

He lowered his head.

She came around to stand in front of him so he was forced to look into a flushed and beautiful face, one full of hurt and anger and questions. So many questions he could not answer.

"You're leaving?"

"I am."

"Forever?"

"I..." His breath shuddered in him. "I think so." He squeezed his eyes but it didn't block out the pain or the sight of her face. He would never forget her face. "I don't know. I have to figure some things out."

"Just like that? You will kiss me like you love me. *Love me*." She pointed at his chest. "And then walk away?" Her wide eyes grew wider by the second and her voice louder.

When he didn't answer, she waved her hand in the air. "What kind of man are you? Who treats a woman that way? And you've been courting me? Except you weren't officially. No wonder you haven't spoken to the duke. You've been playing with me?" Her hurt turned to anger, and her cheeks flushed further. She stepped closer. "Say something."

And then His Grace made his way down the stairs, tying a robe around his waist. "What is the meaning of this?"

Charity dipped her head to see past Andrew up the stairs. "Wilfred kissed me. And then he told me he is not free. And now he's leaving." The desperation in her voice tore at him. He shook his head. But before he could deny her words, he knew that they were true. Was his intent different than the bald face words sounded? Certainly. But nothing could be said to counter her words.

"Lord Lockhart?" His Grace joined them at the base of the stairs.

"She speaks the truth."

Charity seemed to wilt in front of him.

"I think it's time we moved this meeting into my study."

Charity put her hands on His Grace's arm and leaned into him while they walked.

He followed His Grace.

THE TENDER REGARD between them was somewhat surprising to Andrew. But he was pleased she had someone in her life to care for her. He winced. When Lord Morley or the Duke of Granbury found out about this, he might be facing pistols truly.

A new wild exhilaration filled him. Had his actions required that he now marry Charity? Run from Penny and her mother and do his duty here?

The duke entered, leading Charity at his side around to the other side of the desk, sat her next to him, and then turned to Andrew. "Close the door."

JEN GEIGLE JOHNSON

He nodded, did as he was told and then sat in the chair indicated.

His Grace stared at Andrew for what seemed like an eternity and then said, "Explain yourself."

Oh, this was unexpected. He'd have almost preferred a great sermon, a yelling fit, bold accusations. All torture he deserved. But to have to say words that cut him like a knife, that was exquisite pain indeed.

"I didn't plan for any of this to happen."

The duke's eyes sharpened, but he said nothing.

"Last night, after Almack's, a woman and her mother were waiting for me in my front room."

"Is she pregnant?" The duke's overly calm face was unnerving.

Charity's gasp entered his chest and tightened things further.

He knew he crumpled in front of them. He daren't look at Charity. But he cleared his throat. "They are in such a state as to most desperately need my protection."

"And their claim on you?"

He nodded, knowing they would think the worst, but knowing he had to be completely honest. "They have come seeking I act in honor."

Charity's hand went up to her mouth. "This is the man you are?"

"No, Charity."

"You are not at liberty to use her first name." The duke shook his head. "You have used her ill in setting expectations, acting dishonorably, not approaching me and yet monopolizing her time, setting expectations in the ton, limiting her options, and raising her hopes. If you have been so fortunate as to capture her heart, you have now broken it as well. If I

108

believed in pistols, you might be facing mine tomorrow morning." He opened his drawer, and Andrew shrunk back a moment.

"You will leave this house and never return." He pulled out a paper.

"What is that?"

"This is the beginnings of my invitations to the top families in the ton with men who have come seeking an opportunity to win her hand. They will be in my home now, not you. They will be given opportunities to win her heart. Not you. They have behaved honorably as you should have done." He pulled a bell rope.

When the servant stepped inside, Andrew stood.

"Please show this man out."

He looked to Charity, but her eyes stared back in disbelief.

His tongue was bound. He could not say what he wished. He could not destroy the reputation of another to serve his purposes. And he knew he must do his duty by them. For they had no one else.

But to have Charity think ill of him was the cruelest fate of it all. And he knew he'd never forget the horror in her expression. He knew the new masked indifference would be his reception if they were to ever cross paths again.

His feet moved slowly. He could not make them leave the floor. At length his shuffling brought him to the front door, and he stepped outside into the brisk air.

CHAPTER 10

The horror, the complete desperation on Lord Lockhart's face stayed with her. She'd never seen a person so tortured. The power of his kiss, the haunted sorrow in his face, were the only things preventing her from hating the man. All that day and the next and the next, Charity walked about as if in a dream. Callers filled Her Grace's front drawing room, seeking Charity's attention. Flowers covered surfaces. And Charity could feel nothing. The duchess stuck by her side for which Charity should be grateful, but now and then a sigh or cluck followed by silence from the older woman would all but drive Charity to distraction. Did she wish for an alliance with Lord Lockhart? Was she pitying Charity? What did the woman want? Charity never asked her though, because as maddening as it was to guess, she didn't really want to know.

She didn't want to know the sick news behind why Lord Lockhart was behaving as he was. She remembered the letter he'd received, the claim from childhood. Was he simply feeling misplaced responsibility for that woman? To her mother? But then why hadn't he answered straight away about the woman not being pregnant? Why leave the Duke with that understanding? She would be tortured by the unknowns as much as she wished not to know them.

She and the duchess rode together to the new school. Lord Lockhart had secured a location for them. And Charity suspected he'd also been responsible for paying the lease. Their committee would meet now to clear the area and begin collecting books and other necessaries in order for their school to begin. Everything was coming together wonderfully. Charity wished she could find a bit of satisfaction in it, some emotion other than hopeful dread that she might see Lord Lockhart again.

Hopeful dread. Was that a valid emotion? To hope something as much as she dreaded it, certainly felt very real to her.

They arrived to a room full of their volunteers busy doing wonderful things.

And Charity wished she could feel the joy on their faces. After sweeping a bit and walking about aimlessly telling people they were doing a great work, Charity knew she needed something different. The hand she placed on the duchess' arm was clinging and desperate. "Might we go to the park?"

"Certainly. Everything here seems to be wonderfully organized."

"Yes, it does."

Several footmen remained to aid in protection for the women. They were in a relatively safe location, but footmen would always be needed.

As soon as they sat in the carriage, the duchess turned to her. "I know you're unhappy."

Charity nodded.

"I am as well. I really thought that Lord Lockhart, that he…"

Charity looked out the window. "I know."

They said no more until they stopped at the park. "Wait for us." The duchess descended first.

When Charity linked arms with her, she was filled again with an appreciation for her kindness. "I have found in you a true friend and ally."

"Yes. Perhaps you thought we would be an unlikely pair in the beginning."

Charity smiled remembering their early days of receiving charity from the woman and her rival, the Duchess of Sussex. "I admit to being surprised to learn of your bluestocking ways."

"We're a snobby lot, aren't we?"

Charity was surprised into a laugh. "The bluestockings? How so?"

"We only truly respect those who we view to be of higher intelligence. The other pursuits of women are beneath us and as a result, so are they."

"Too true, and yet, I'd not like to think of myself in such a manner."

"It's self-preservation. But I think you are correct in that it's a baser way of thinking. There is room in our society for all sorts."

Charity leaned closer, holding the duchess' arm in an embrace. "And yet, all women are remarkable. They're intelligent. Whether they choose to use their talents to find a man and further his and her social standing or to building schools and feeding orphans. Women can do all manner of things." She leaned over and kissed the duchess right on the cheek.

"They can gift gowns to impoverished sisters and pay them visits so that they remain relevant in their class."

The duchess turned shining eyes to Charity. "Yes, they can."

They walked along, enjoying a hazy sort of wet day. Charity felt her heart begin to be comforted.

Just as she reached to run fingers along a hedgerow, the duchess stopped in her tracks, pulling Charity close. "See there."

Lord Lockhart stepped out from one of the many walking paths with a small bit of a woman on his arm, and what looked to be her mother at the woman's side. All of Charity's comforting balm squelched into a tightened mass of angst. "Ooh. And there they are." She frowned.

"Shall we watch a moment to see if we learn something about this most odd of all circumstances?"

"Yes." Neither seemed at all concerned at their blatant spying.

Lord Lockhart seemed pleased enough, if not happy necessarily; he smiled and answered with attention to both the woman and her mother.

The woman turned so that her profile was most visible and then for a moment, her hand curled around her abdomen.

The duchess gasped, and Charity clung to her as though she might faint.

"She is with child. It's true." The duchess shook her head. "All this time I couldn't believe it. I wouldn't. Our Lord Lockhart..." She clucked. "But here he is. Here she is. And there is no mistake." She stood taller. "And now, you must decide something."

Charity could hardly think through the thoughts that swam in front of her eyes. With child? Lord Lockhart's? Nothing made sense to her. But the duchess demanded attention, so she blinked away some of her confusion and focused. "What must I decide?"

"Are you going to walk away and pretend you never saw this meeting? Or are you going to make yourself known and loudly?" She nodded her head toward a group of men approaching on the same path as Lord Lockhart.

They were within calling distance and certainly within walking distance. Charity looked from them to Lord Lockhart and back. Then Lord Wessex's laugh carried over to her, and her decision was made.

The duchess picked up her feet, and they hurried as quickly as she'd ever seen Her Grace move in the direction of the approaching lords.

When they were close enough, Charity stepped into their path and set her hand on Lord Wessex's arm.

They all stopped immediately, bowing to the duchess and then to Charity.

Lord Wessex grinned in such a natural manner, Charity was tempted to reconsider her opinions of him. "And to what do I owe this sudden pleasure of your company?"

She laughed. "You have come at the perfect time. Her Grace and I were just bemoaning our lack of escort." She stood closer and fluttered her eyelashes. Astounded at how easily the role of flirt was becoming, she laughed again when his eyebrow rose high on his head.

"Oh stop. I'm pleased to see you. Is that so unbelievable?"

"Not at all. I've been hoping for just such a boon." He turned to the others. "Men, what say you? Are we man enough to escort women such as these?"

"We certainly are." One of the younger lords held his arm out for the duchess. "If I may?"

"I would be most grateful. Thank you, young man."

"And now we are off in the direction of…ices? The tea room?"

"Tea would be lovely." Charity nodded.

"Quite right," the duchess added from behind them.

"Tea room it is." They began their walk again, and Lord Wessex put a hand over hers. "Perhaps you are beginning to see that we could be merry together."

A loud giggle carried over to them from Lord Lockhart's group. Charity stiffened. And Lord Wessex's gaze sharpened. "Or perhaps you are merely tasting the spoils of a loss?" He shook his head. "We can't have that." Then he directed their steps toward Lord Lockhart.

"What are you doing?"

"I think a few comparisons are in order."

"How so?"

"The kind that will show you that you are in finer company indeed."

"That is not necessary. I don't know why you think I should even care for other company than yours."

"We shall see then, shall we?" They were almost close enough for Lord Lockhart to hear.

"Must we?" She felt her knees shake in a ridiculous fashion. Lord Lockhart's gaze was locked on her.

"Just as I suspected. You are affected by him. And he has chosen another. You feel spurned which is utterly ridiculous being the exquisite creature that you are and him being…him. Yes, we must approach them. Now come, this shall be deliciously fun. You'll see."

She studied the situation. Lord Lockhart, his pregnant woman, her mother. And who was in Charity's party? A rather large handful of lords and the Duchess of York. She stood taller. Yes, perhaps this would not be as painful as she'd predicted. She held her head a touch higher.

"There you go, now come, we must be having the most merry of times, and you must be more enamored." He leaned in closer. "Perhaps if I should behave in a more tempting manner, you should feel more in the mood." His mouth moved closer, almost brushing her skin, his breath a puff of a presence near her ear.

"Lord Wessex." She stepped away.

"Come now, you enjoy it. I can see it on your skin, in your eyes, by the smile playing across your full mouth."

"It's not without its pleasures, but surely you are too bold, the situation too observed."

"Ah yes. But no harm done, subtleties matter in situations such as these, and we've not even touched."

He had a point. Perhaps a moot point—if the entire ton thought they were together, then it wouldn't matter what arguments they brought to the table. And there was the obvious problem that she didn't feel altogether comfortable with him so close, his lips so close.

The women had now noticed their approach, and she stood closer to Lord Lockhart. The possessive hand the younger woman placed on his arm was at last all the motivation Charity needed to step closer to Lord Wessex, to smile as though he were amusing and act as though she did not know she was walking closer and closer to Lord Lockhart, whose eyes had not diverted from staring right at her.

When they were at last in front of the group, hers crowding in—an abundance of men, the Duchess of York, and herself, she forced herself to look at Lord Lockhart.

Lord Wessex laughed. "Lockhart."

"Wessex." He barely spoke the name, his teeth clenched tightly together.

An awkward moment followed while they all stared at the woman at his side until she shook his arm, subtly, but noticeably.

"Oh, forgive me. This is Miss Penny." The smile he sent her was kind but not loving. "Her mother, Mrs. Westchester." He turned to them.

"This is Miss Charity." The tone, the expression in his eyes, the deference he gave to Charity about stole her breath. Gone was the kindness, replaced by the intensity of their moments in the kitchen, by the love that flowed between them. She found it difficult to know how to respond. She gripped Lord Wessex's arm as though she might faint straight away.

Once introductions were made, Lord Wessex lifted a hand. "We are off to the tea room. Would you like to join us?"

Miss Penny said yes while Lord Lockhart said no.

Which made Lord Wessex laugh. "Well then, perhaps we shall see you there." He nodded to Charity. "Shall we?"

"Yes, please."

She felt a bit like she was leaving Lord Lockhart on a deserted island without water to drink. But she forced herself not to turn again to see his face.

One of the lords behind them called out. "Was it just me, or was that unnecessarily awkward?"

Everyone laughed, but Lord Wessex leaned closer. "You did well. The first meeting is always the most difficult."

She let his words settle for a moment, bringing some semblance of comfort. "Will it get easier?"

"Certainly. With every subsequent meeting and the more time you spend with me." His eyes were kind which surprised her. But his words were incredibly arrogant. She did not know how to mesh the two into a person she understood.

But they continued on their walk toward the tea room, and in truth, the further they walked from Lord Lockhart, the better she felt.

Safe from his love, from the desperation in his expression.

But not really safe from her own love that burned just as brightly as ever, so brightly she doubted very much that she'd ever feel recovered from such an allegiance.

CHAPTER 11

*L*ord Lockhart stared at the brandy on his sideboard in the study, the only room in the house free of Mrs. Westchester and her daughter.

Was he already hiding from them? Yes, he was.

The renovations and decorating of his home had already begun. Every new drape, every new cover for his chairs, every new paint color filled his home with Charity. There was not a room in the place that did not remind him of her, that did not tug at him to call at her house, to spend time at the school with the hopes that she would be there, to fall at her feet in apology. Even his study, which as yet had no memories of Miss Penny, had snippets of Charity. And he wished to keep his sanctuary sacred.

But a knock at the door and Penny's soft voice on the other side had him leaping to his feet. He opened the door and closed it behind him before she could step foot in his space. "Yes?"

She stepped back, eyeing him with suspicion. "Oh, I wondered if you would like some company? This morning

119

has been so quiet, and Mother is intent on her needlepoint." She looked around his shoulder at the closed door. "I do not wish to disturb your work, just perhaps join you, with a book?"

He nodded, slowly. Of course she would be bored. Naturally he had a responsibility to entertain his guests. His aunt had taken to hiding in her rooms. It was no secret that she was not pleased with the new developments, nor did she enjoy the company of the Westchesters.

"Perhaps we could tour a museum?"

Her face lit. "I'd like that. Before I start…" Her hand went down to her stomach. "I would enjoy some outings of some kind."

Before she started *showing*. The words shook him. The reality of his situation hammered home even further. He knew it would behoove him to get a special license. Or to at least have the marriage banns read. They needed to marry swiftly to give them the least disfavor from Society as possible. Truly, he should probably return home.

But he couldn't do any of those things, not yet. He didn't have the force of will.

"If you could summon your maid, let's pay a visit to the museum." He'd been wanting to see a new exhibit. And he'd been most interested in a set of scrolls someone had donated. Perhaps they would let him have a look at them.

Mrs. Westchester bustled into the front area as they were about to leave. "Oh, I'm so pleased. Seeing the two of you together, making merry like you used to, it gives me hope for our future together."

His and Penny's smiles were matching as they attempted to feign the same amount of energy that Mrs. Westchester poured in an overabundance over them all.

When at last in the carriage, they both breathed out in relief.

And then she laughed. "I apologize for Mother."

"No need."

"I wish I could say her enthusiasm would lessen."

"But we would both know you were lying."

"Too true."

He studied her face. Perhaps they could make a decent time of it. Certainly, honesty would be required. "Tell me about him."

Her gaze shot to his face, pain filling her expression. And then she shook her head.

"Why not? Tell me."

"Do you feel comfortable telling me about her?"

A sharp stabbing feeling in his chest brought her message home. "Not yet."

She nodded and looked away. The silence between them lingered, but he didn't press her. After so long he thought she had given up speaking altogether, her quiet voice carried over to him. "He is an honorable man."

Andrew doubted very much that could be true, given her circumstances.

"You don't believe me." Her eyes fired an accusation, daring him to deny her.

"How could I? When here I am, doing the honorable thing by you that he should be doing?"

"Mother wouldn't let him."

Andrew's eyebrow rose, challenging her.

"You think I should have done as I pleased, Mother's opinion aside." Her statement sounded tired. As if she'd thought the very thing a thousand times. And he imagined she had.

"I do. Or perhaps not gotten yourself into such a situation. Again, an honorable man would not have done this to you."

Pain filled her eyes, and she looked away. "That's where you are wrong."

He didn't wish to discuss it further. He was more inclined to hear about the man's hobbies, or inclination to laugh overly loud, or some such thing.

"You don't want to marry me."

He sighed.

And nothing more was said.

But the museum arrived, and they would now be in front of others. "You are my first friend. I don't want to marry you in the sense that I would long for a wife, but I want to marry you in the sense that you came to me in need, and I am honored to do what I can."

She nodded. "Thank you."

He stepped down and turned to reach for her hand. "Shall we see the exhibits?"

"Yes." Her face cheered somewhat. "At last to be out of that house, with all the new touches Miss Charity made over the place."

His eyes shot to hers. "Do you not approve of the changes?"

"No, they're perfect. Am I to think of her whenever we are in London?"

He would be thinking of her whenever they were anywhere.

And the wrongness of his situation started to tug at him. What was right here? To marry and pine for another as they would both do? To not marry and allow a friend to be ruined?

Her voice interrupted his thoughts. "Many a person marries for reasons other than love. And surely they have their heart tugged in other directions. We shall not be so different from them."

"Not at all different I imagine."

"Except there will be a child."

A child that wasn't his. If it was a son, was this person to be his heir? Could he love the little person as it deserved to be?

"You say the most difficult things when we are surrounded by others and I cannot respond."

"I know. Perhaps I'm afraid to hear what you would say if we were alone and you were free to speak your mind."

Her hand rested on his forearm but he received no pleasure in it. Still, they had been friends for many years. "Remember the tree that I always bested you at climbing?"

"Oh no. We are not going to let that stand. I bested you. For years. One time. One tiny time, I stumbled and you raced to the top first."

"But it was the final time. And therefore stands as the winning moment."

"We shall have to climb it again. I see that only then will you desist in claiming such a preposterous win."

He laughed. It felt good to come to a meeting point about their earlier friendship. Her mother was right. The strength of that friendship might help them to manage the other difficulties that were bound to come.

He patted her hand in appreciation for those memories.

And then a laugh interrupted his momentary pleasantries.

Her laugh.

Charity entered the same room as they from the opposite corner. She was even more beautiful than the last time he'd seen her. She'd taken to dressing exquisitely all the time instead of just when the duchess made her. And the effect was…nothing short of dazzling. Everyone in the room turned to her. And most eyes stayed put, following her as she and Lord Wessex approached the first painting.

Suddenly, all Andrew wanted was to hear her thoughts on the artist's representation. He wanted to hear her thoughts on all things. She always had a thought. She was never bent on hiding them, and he missed every clever and outrageous thing she was bound to say.

Even though Miss Penny stiffened beside him, he moved them quickly closer with the hope that he might hear some of her cleverness.

They arrived close enough for him to hear her laugh, a real sound, like she was enjoying herself. Her hand rested on Lord Wessex's arm. They stood close. And he looked oddly attentive. Gone were his rakish attentions replaced more by…respect.

He regretted his actions immediately and wished to be as far from them as possible.

Lord Wessex nodded. "And this one looks to be similar to his others in color, but I can't help but think he is attempting something more right here." He pointed to something on the painting. Andrew leaned to the side to have a better view.

Penny huffed beside him. She crossed her arms, staring at him.

He whispered, "I'm interested in this painting."

"And the people standing in front of it."

"Yes," he told her unabashedly. "I'm interested in what they have to say."

Charity turned eyes up to Lord Wessex's that looked to hold equal respect. "I think perhaps this use of light here and this cluster of peasants near is representing a new beginning?" Her gaze flickered to Andrew and away, the briefest motion, but enough for him to want to clutch at his heart and turn away. It entered straight inside. A new beginning. Without him. His beginning already begun with Miss Penny. His and Charity's lives diverging from each other, not quite gone, but almost. What would he do about it? Would he stand helplessly by?

Charity and Lord Wessex turned the other direction and stopped in front of the next painting. And all Andrew could do was watch in agony as he lost her.

Penny cleared her throat.

After a long breath, he turned to her. "I'm woolgathering, aren't I?"

"Is that what you're doing?"

"Yes. I believe that's what it's called when your mind wanders." He needed to stop and converse with politeness the woman he was planning to marry. The words choked their way into his mind. *Marry.*

"I suppose I'd do the same if Auggie were here."

That was the first time she'd said his name. Auggie. It seemed fitting. "But he will be near when we return to my estate." He studied her. He knew many people had side relationships while married as long as the heir and another were thriving and well, but he'd never wanted a marriage like that. And even given the circumstances, he did not want a marriage like that now.

She shook her head, her face suddenly bright pink.

"Apologies." He glanced around them.

"We aren't…we don't…"

The crowd was growing. People moved past them in both directions. "Might we go elsewhere to have such a discussion?"

She nodded.

But Lord Wessex returned at that moment and lifted a hand in their direction.

Andrew stood taller and braced himself.

The look Charity sent his way was worse than if she'd just ignored him outright. She'd mastered the indifferent mask. And he suddenly wished to shock it from her face.

"Lockhart."

"Wessex."

"We were just on our way out and wondered if you'd like to join us?"

"Oh? Where are we going?"

"I thought for a ride in the park? I have my phaeton, and the weather promises to be enjoyable."

A group of ladies passed by, every one of them eyeing Lord Wessex with expectant eyes, but the man didn't seem to notice them. Had he truly reformed his ways? Charity was enough of a prize to turn any man's heart for good. Perhaps she'd succeed with his. But Andrew didn't trust him. Not one bit. And he didn't want Charity's heart caught up in his. From what he'd heard, Wessex would stick around only long enough to know he'd made another conquest.

But what could Andrew say? He had already used her most ill and might have broken her heart already.

She looked up into Lord Wessex's face as if sharing a secret.

Though she seemed to have recovered remarkably quickly.

Everything seemed too difficult at the moment. He was obviously willing to do good for his childhood friend, but obviously not completely since he could hardly bear to think the words. He'd hurt his most dearest love and pushed her into the arms of the biggest rake in all of London, and a part of him could not let her go, and he certainly couldn't let her be hurt by this cad of a person. But his childhood best friend was in the direst straits. And as of yet, he'd not been able to think of any solution for her besides the one that forced him to marry her and destroy all of their happiness.

He bit back a sigh and nodded. "I think we'd enjoy a ride in the park. Penny hasn't had a good view of it this visit."

"Or ever." She fluttered her eyelashes. "This is my first time in London."

"Is it?" Lord Wessex grinned. "Well, then we shall have to give the longer tour for Miss Penny, what say you?" He turned to Andrew who could only nod.

Two couples with very little to say to each other moved toward the front door of the museum out onto the street and then toward the phaeton.

Lord Wessex laughed when he handed Charity up. "It might be cozy, but I'm sure none of us will complain."

He handed up Miss Penny next and then climbed up himself, leaving Andrew to wedge himself in after, with only Lord Wessex to converse with.

"Nice pair you have."

"Thank you. The bays are high-stepping and will promenade. These aren't the best for racing."

"Surely a better use for them here in the park, much more promenading certainly, than racing."

"Yes, and if I really want to race, I can borrow Lord Fellon's racing horses."

Andrew nodded.

Right when he resigned himself to having to make mindless conversation with this man for the entirety of the ride, Lord Wessex surprised him by beginning a conversation with Miss Penny.

"So, your first time in London?"

Her responding giggle also surprised Andrew as he'd never heard her giggle, ever, not in all his years of knowing her as a girl.

His gaze caught Charity's, and for a moment their circumstances were forgotten and the look of disbelief at the growing flirtation between Lord Wessex and Miss Penny gifted them with solidarity.

Then when Lord Wessex adjusted his arm so that it would more easily fit along the back of their bench, around Miss Penny, Andrew snorted and leaned forward.

Charity did the same.

For a moment, their shared glance spoke many things that neither could voice. "Are you well?" he at last asked.

She almost nodded but then shook her head. The pain that rushed into her expression was too much for him and obviously for her because she looked away.

Their moment lost, he shifted his wedged self again, attempting some form of comfort. And then Miss Penny laughed out loud with an accompanying hiccup. "You are so funny. Lord Wessex, I haven't enjoyed myself this much in ages."

And Andrew had had enough. More for Charity's sake than his own, he tapped the man on the knee, reaching for the reins. "Might I have a go?"

"Oh, certainly." He handed over the reins, and Andrew winked at Charity before a sharp snap with them on the horses' backs gave him great satisfaction. They leapt forward, causing a sharp scream from Miss Penny and a "Whoa, man what are you thinking?" from Lord Wessex.

"Come now, man. A little diversion is needed, don't you think?" The dare in his face silenced Lord Wessex, and the man's attention was diverted from Miss Penny to more acutely watching the paths to their front.

The horses' pace quickened again, and Andrew led them to rarely used paths. They flew along hedgerows, and then out across an expansive green, until he circled back toward the more populated parts of the park and slowed the horses again.

"Exhilarating." He grinned. "Thank you for the ride, Lord Wessex. This is where Miss Penny and I must descend. Unfortunately."

"Oh yes, certainly." Lord Wessex stopped the horses altogether and then Andrew leapt down, helping Miss Penny after.

Charity did not meet his gaze from her now-roomy spot on the phaeton, but her lips battled a smile and for that, the outing was worth his time.

After watching them move forward and away for a brief moment, he offered his arm to Miss Penny. "That was something."

"Yes, it was." She said little, and when he began to suspect she might keep her lips tightly locked for the remainder of their walk, he cleared his throat. "You were friendly with Lord Wessex."

"Oh? He's a friendly type of person, isn't he?" Her cheeks colored a bit.

"And Auggie?"

Then she paled and looked away, her breath catching. "Must you persist in bringing him up?"

"Mustn't I?"

"I don't see how he signifies at all in any of our conversations."

"Except that he's your love…or is he?"

"What is that supposed to mean?"

"I just don't know how you can profess to love one but hope to be engaged to another and then flirt shamelessly with yet another." He stared at her profile which she refused to turn.

She picked up her pace, releasing his arm.

And he didn't attempt to match her hurrying feet.

But she was shorter than he and her small steps did not find her moving too great a distance ahead.

They continued thus through the rest of the park, Andrew attempting to make her out and she refusing to give any hints.

He didn't know what to think of his old friend. But one thing he did know and that was he was relieved he had not yet proposed. And even if before they were feeling an urgency to rush the engagement, he was not, not anymore.

CHAPTER 12

*C*harity's dissatisfaction grew. Her sorrow continued. And she found less and less relief from her efforts to numb the pain. Flirting with Lord Wessex, attempting to find another marriage match when her heart was not in the effort, both wore on her. The fatigue and the ache in her head at night were evidence of her unhappiness. This morning, when the ache continued, Charity knew she had to do something different. But what could a person do when they loved someone who had done such terrible things?

"Perhaps I should just return home." Thoughts of their castle, the lovely grounds, the sea that stretched out in a great blue from the cliffs to the horizon, filled her with longing.

But no one could hear her. At least any servants busy about their tasks gave no indication. She made her way down to breakfast. She had but a moment to grab a biscuit before Lord Wessex would be there with the carriage. They were to tour the home of a visiting royal. The home had been redecorated for the lease, and tours were being offered to a limited select few.

Apparently this woman, a French princess, was on good terms with Lord Wessex.

Charity sighed. She was kidding herself if she did not know in what manner he had found himself on good terms with the woman.

She needed her sisters.

The Duchess of York was sitting at the table when Charity entered.

"Oh, I'm pleased to see you this morning."

"Thank you. You as well." Her words sounded flat to her own ears. She hoped she would not offend Her Grace. "How are you this morning?"

"I've been missing you. Your outings with Lord Wessex are such that I am not as involved in them."

"I imagine that's true." She searched her hostess' face. "Do you disapprove of him?"

The sigh in response sounded deep and heavy. And the subsequent pause felt lengthy. At last, she rested her hands on the table. "I approved of him as a friendly distraction, as someone who would surely never settle down himself."

"And now?"

"Now, I don't know. Is he tending toward the more serious? The loyal?" Her eyebrows lifted in such a dubious expression, that Charity could only agree with her.

"After our ride in the park, I would say he is only partially loyal."

"And how do you feel about that?"

She'd asked herself that question often over the past day or two, and after their ride today, she knew the answer. "I don't think it matters much to me at all as I don't plan on tying myself to him in any way."

The duchess nodded. And then her eyes turned sad. "I still cannot understand how such a good man could be…not as good as we thought. He was so in love. He doted on you. I was certain he was about to propose, he…" She sighed again.

"We're talking about Lord Lockhart now."

"Of course. And as much as we might wish to avoid the man, we have to get this school up and running."

Charity nodded. "Have I forgotten another meeting?"

"Almost."

"Today?"

"Yes, we are meeting at the school, and we need materials."

Her heart skipped. She'd forgotten. The school. "Oh yes. I'm…I'm going to deliver those." She picked up a biscuit. She would do it. But first she had to meet Lord Wessex.

Her Grace lifted a book from her lap up onto the table. "I've been reading this."

Charity moved closer. "Is that…?"

"The Treatise on Women."

She could hardly resist that literature. Lord Wessex would have to wait. "And what do you think?" She moved a chair closer to sit right beside her. "Have you read the parts about suffrage?"

"Yes, certainly. And the declaration that every woman has intelligence." She nodded. "As much as a man." Her eyes gleamed. "I always knew it to be true."

"Me too."

Her Grace opened the book and began reading her favorite passages.

Soon Charity was as lost in the book as she ever had been. The duchess's finger shook as she followed lines and turned pages. "I've been wondering, hoping some of this could be true."

Charity nodded. "It is true. This part. Right here." She leaned closer as words sunk deep inside her, words she'd read before but had forgotten in the haze of her heartbreak, in the haze of finding false satisfaction in the company of men like Lord Wessex, in the idea that she must marry someone, not mattering at all who.

Women and men are equal in soul, intelligence, and nobility of soul. And each has a strength and purpose all their own. Her wit, rational power and speech make her excel in all duties that are uniquely hers.

"How often do you hear words like that?" The duchess laughed.

"Never." Charity smiled. "Every woman needs to hear these words, and often."

"Do you ever think about how odd it is that these very words are so important but prevented even by other women? Some shun and mistreat other women who would champion their cause. Bluestockings? What else do they call us? And why? Are we afraid to be strong? Are we afraid when other women are strong? I don't know, Your Grace. But I wish that every woman knew just those simple words we just read, and so many others, but those at the very least." She sat back, astounded that she could be so caught up in unimportant things for so long. "And I've been spending time doing what? Trying to impress men who I don't even like?" She shook her head. "You have been very kind, but I care much more about this right here." She pointed her finger down on the book. "Than I do about a lifetime of marriage to the wrong person."

The duchess turned to her with fiery eyes. "But my dear, the right man might not be what we think. And he's taken."

"Then would it be so wrong to never marry? Or at least not to marry until I've met someone I respect and love again?" The words almost stuck in her throat. She had not desired to marry anyone but Lord Lockhart, except, not the Lord Lockhart that had been responsible for Miss Penny's pregnancy. Oh goodness. The Lord Lockhart that likely didn't exist. The man who would never do such a thing, the man who was smart and purposeful and kind and …. Who loved her.

"But you'll have to marry."

"My sisters will care for me. And I'll write treatises like this one. I'll start publishing like Kate, only I'll discuss matters of understanding for women."

"You will always be welcome here, my dear."

"Thank you, Your Grace."

"And don't give up on marriage yet. We still have a Season to complete. We must never underestimate the power of a London Season to see someone in love and married off."

Charity laughed even though she knew the marriage mart was not for her.

The butler entered. "A Lord Wessex to see you, Miss Charity."

When the duchess groaned beside her, Charity rested a hand on her arm. "Don't you worry, Your Grace." She stood.

Lord Wessex bowed to them both and when Charity had risen from her curtsey, she hurried to him. "Oh, I'm so glad you're early. Would you mind terribly if we stopped at the school first? We have some items to deliver there."

"The school? Certainly."

"Thank you." She tucked her hands into his arm. He was a good enough sort of man as long as she wasn't in love with him. Pity the woman who lost her heart to him.

As they pulled up to the school and all the committee was there helping, she could only feel a great exhilaration about the project. Everywhere she looked, she saw the cute little girl, Ronda, who'd tried to pickpocket. And she hoped to be able to help many more just like her.

CHAPTER 13

*C*harity marched into the ball in the same way she had many times before she'd started acting like a marriage mart debutante. She moved to her favorite corner and started talking about the school. They were in need of a few more donations and hands to help and besides those two purposes, she simply wished to talk about something of substance.

Before too long Lord Granville joined her. "Are you back, then?" His eyes smiled at her.

"Yes, I am, and the children at the schoolhouse could use your support."

"Excellent." He grinned. "Tell me all about them."

Ohers joined. And soon she was happier than she'd been in a long time. "And my lords, that is how you keep your job security."

"Our job security?"

"Certainly. You've seen all these riots? They're not going to be throwing tomatoes at the ones that vote for change."

Music for a new song started up. And this time, instead of

the whole group uniformly ignoring it, much preferring conversations, they paused, and three lords at once reached for her hand asking her to dance.

She clucked. "Really, you think we should be dancing at a time like this?"

"Well, Miss Charity. We are at a ball. We can converse in the line, can we not?" Lord Granville held out his hand.

"Oh, very well. Shall I dance with the lot of you then?"

The resounding affirmative answers confounded her. "Right then. But I want to see each one of you at the school come tomorrow morning and every day this week."

Lord Wessex approached. "Might I have the supper set?" He dipped his head, his eyes drinking her in as if she were the most important person in the room.

She wished to fan her face. That Lord Wessex really understood what most men did not—that a woman valued being seen—was his most important asset.

"Yes, you may."

"I shall be counting the moments until then."

She laughed. "And so shall I."

When she turned back to Lord Granville, he was studying her with a serious expression.

"Now, what's this?"

"His reputation leaves room for everything he says to be suspect. For you to be held in disregard alongside him, forgive my bold manner in speaking."

He led her out onto the floor.

"And what about you? What is your motivation for asking me to dance?" She curtseyed before him in the line.

"My motivation is simply to enjoy your company, support your causes and learn from you."

She raised an eyebrow.

"If you were the least bit interested in me in any other way, I would be most pleased, but I know your heart is not inclined toward me. Or at least I don't have the wiles to win you over like some."

"That manner of expertise is not needed." She moved toward him and then away, following the steps in the dance. He'd long been high on her list of most eligible men of her acquaintance. "If I was seeking merely a marriage of people who get on well together, I'd wish for you to speak with the duke right away."

They each faced the next person in line and would be apart for many more moments in the dance. Charity's mind was a jumble of emotion and thoughts. She didn't know how to move forward. Lord Wessex was not the man to make her happy, though he was certainly expert in his methods of wooing a woman. Lord Granville would be an excellent match. She could encourage him. She could get on well with him. He appreciated her conversation and her desire to do good. She turned in a circle, moving toward whoever was next in line and suddenly she was facing Lord Lockhart.

She gasped in a painful breath. Captured by his gaze, she could only stare up into his face, her hands and feet doing whatever they did, she hardly knew.

"Charity." Her name breathed out of his lips as though long unspoken, as though he hungered for the sound.

"Wilfred."

His lips twitched. And the spell was broken.

She circled round him, their hands touched, and she moved on. But every part of her was changed. And she knew why she couldn't be satisfied with Lord Granville. She could never be happy with anyone but Lord Lockhart.

When she was at last facing Lord Granville again, he

dipped his head. "But your heart is captured by another." His gaze flicked to Lord Lockhart and back to her.

"Who is not free to return the love."

His eyes widened. "And so there is hope for me still." His smile grew, and with one wiggle of his eyebrow, she laughed.

They ended the dance, laughing about nonsensical things, and she could only be grateful for his distraction from her moments with Lord Lockhart.

Two partners later, the music for the supper set began, and Lord Wessex bowed in front of her. "And now, my most anticipated dance."

She curtseyed low. She enjoyed his attention. She liked the way he made her feel. But she knew his smiles and his compliments were not just for her.

They moved in and out of the more challenging dance steps. Every time they came together, he said some snippet of some flowery compliment, never quite finishing a phrase until they at last had a few longer moments while they waited for the next couple to finish a step. "And this will not do. Might I have the next waltz, whenever it may be?"

She laughed. "This does not allow for conversation, does it?"

"Not at all, and yours is highly valued."

They stepped together and apart, Charity wishing the words he said were true and sincere. "Can you mean such things?"

"Of course I mean them."

"But you must know that particular compliment would mean more to me than others."

"More than the times I tell you you are the most beautiful woman in the room?"

"Yes more than those, and the others."

"The ones where I say you have captured my attention, no other can compare. The incomparable Charity Standish."

"Yes, I've heard that one as well, but you must know which I most highly value."

He dipped his head. "I have paid much attention to you. I know what you value. And yes, I know you most appreciate good conversation." They stood close for a moment and he whispered in her ear. "But it doesn't mean I don't mean every word."

They stepped apart, and she was left pondering his words. She decided he did mean every word. But perhaps he meant every word to every woman he spoke to.

They finished that set and moved into the dining hall. She sat across from Lord Wessex.

"Do you need more lemonade?"

"Oh yes, I'd like that, if you don't mind."

"I'll be right back." She watched his handsome retreating form. Many female eyes watched him, some overtly, some in disguise behind their fans. He was not a welcome sight for many a mother in that room. And Charity could well see why. She was well on her way to being enamored with the man's company, not really with him necessarily, but with the way he made her feel. And that could be very compelling indeed.

A voice in her ear, and the familiar smells of sandalwood and mint washed over her. She turned to a rather close Lord Lockhart who had just arrived at their table apparently. Miss Penny joined them as well and sat across from him.

"What did you say?" She searched his face.

"I said, your eyes linger on him. Do you want everyone in the room to think you've fallen for his traps?"

She turned away. "What do you know about any of this?"

"Enough to know you don't need to be another one of the conquests he casts aside."

"Like your fiancée?"

His eyes widened and then closed. And she wished to take back her words, but in some way, he deserved them. How dare he speak so intimately to her after the way he'd behaved, after kissing her when he was not free to do so. Still, she did not wish to bring pain.

But he shook his head. "I know. In truth, I do not know what to do." His words were close to her; they sent lovely tingles down her neck. And intrigued her to no end. Was Miss Penny really enamored with Lord Wessex? Surely not more than any other woman, not seriously pursuing him. She was in no state to do so.

The woman in question was currently staring daggers at the two of them, and Charity turned to face her. "Hello, Miss Penny."

"You look lovely this evening."

"Thank you. As do you."

They got through the niceties, the platitudes, and Charity wanted to see if she had any awareness at all about the school.

"I've been telling everyone—I'm sure you've heard—that the school could still use support. In fact, we have openings for volunteers if you would like to join us during the first week."

She shook her head. "While I'm sure you find great satisfaction in such things, I'm not of the same mind. I do not believe educating the poor will do any good for our society."

Charity knew her mouth hung open, but she could do nothing about it, so shocked was she in the response. "How can you say that?"

A soft lift of one shoulder dismissed Charity's question as

though it had no consequence. Then she shook her head. "What will a poor person do with an education? A tenant farmer for example, what will they do? They are still a farmer and there is no way around that and no way out, no matter who they know or how many they love." She cleared her throat. "I just don't see the point in it."

Charity was more and more confused by this woman and why Lord Lockhart had anything at all to do with her, let alone wished to marry her? Have a child with her? Before she could respond, Lord Wessex returned with lemonade. "What is this? Are we to have such enjoyable partners at dinner?"

Miss Penny smiled. "I'm so pleased as well." Her fluttering and smiles seemed not only inappropriate but also insincere. What was she after?

Lord Lockhart seemed nonplussed by it. And his gaze was directed at Charity anyway.

The food came and went with a continuous stream of chatter from Miss Penny to entertain them. Even Lord Wessex seemed to be bored by it after a time. She laughed overly loud for a moment and then her face changed to a ping of discomfort. She turned to Lord Lockhart, who wasn't paying attention to her at all.

Charity nodded in her direction, so he turned. "What is it? Are you well?"

She shook her head. And wrapped her hands around her stomach.

Charity stood. "Shall I fetch your mother?"

"Let her betrothed make such a noble gesture." Lord Wessex eyed Lord Lockhart in what looked almost like a challenge.

"She is not my betrothed. But I'm happy to help. Shall I summon Mrs. Westchester?"

Miss Penny stood. "I shall summon her myself." But she swayed a moment and then gripped the back of her chair.

Lord Wessex leapt forward and caught her mid-swoon.

"Oh goodness."

Lord Lockhart looked as though he might leap over the table, but Lord Wessex waved him away. "Don't upset the glasses." He hefted Miss Penny up into his arms. Many in the room looked to Lord Lockhart and back to Lord Wessex, and the whispers were starting.

"Oh, they're gonna talk about this."

"Has that ever bothered us before?"

"No, but they were discussing our overly educated conversation and our bluestocking ways, all things I view as the highest compliments."

"Too true." He studied her so long she at last turned to face him.

"I'm sorry."

"I know. I just don't know if sorry is going to fix any of this." How could it?

His hand brushed hers and with her gloves off, and his close proximity, she couldn't help but wish he would do it again. She sighed. "Lord Lockhart, what are you doing?"

"I'm...I'm hoping there is still a chance for us."

Her mouth dropped. "How could there be? You would give up your duty? Leave her to fend for herself?" *With your child?* Sitting here, staring him in the face, she still could not fathom how he would have done such a thing. And how she could have been so misguided as to his character. And yet love him all at the same time.

Lord Wessex returned. "She is with her mother, and they are both requesting your carriage."

Lord Lockhart stood. "I forgot for a moment that we came

in my carriage." He bowed to them and then made his way out.

Lord Wessex sat again, across from Charity. "What an interesting couple."

"I find I cannot quite make them out."

"Can't you?"

She shook her head.

The music started, a waltz. And he held out his hand. "And here is my dance."

With some admitted relief from the confusion that was tying her stomach in knots, she placed a hand in his, circled the table and joined him at his side.

They made a good match. If you could judge things like that based on how a couple danced the waltz. They moved in unity. He was exceptional. And she felt as though she were floating. But that was the thing with Lord Wessex. Every moment they spent together she asked herself, is this how every girl feels? Does he use these same methods to win every woman he spends time with?

She suspected that he did.

Halfway through the dance, Lord Wessex whispered in her ear. "I could use some air. Would you mind if we took this set outside on the verandah?"

A bit of reckless daring filled her, ample warnings following soon after. But she nodded. "I'd like that."

He led her out the doors, and she tried to ignore a few knowing stares that followed after them.

She went immediately to the stone railing and leaned over it with her forearms. The cool night air sent waves of refreshing sensations over her skin. For a moment, she said nothing.

Lord Wessex stood beside her. His eyes were on her.

And after a moment, she turned to face him.

"So much is going on in your head all the time. What do you think when you look at me?" He leaned with one hip up against the stone.

She laughed. "What kind of a question is that?"

"The kind that begs an answer."

"Very well. I'm just not certain what to think about you. I see a man who will always be a mystery."

"And do you like mysteries?" His eyes were dark, unreadable.

"I love a good mystery in a book." She shifted. "But in a person, I'm not sure how I feel about not ever knowing…"

"Knowing?" He waited, watching her with his unreadable face, standing close, closer all the time.

"Knowing if I'm your first choice."

He nodded. And then he lifted his hand up to tuck a hair behind her ear. "You have the most fascinating hair."

She crossed her arms.

"But you'd like to know if you're my first choice?"

She looked away. "Actually, I don't know if I'm ready to know something like that."

"That's right. The woman who learns that will receive a marriage proposal shortly after and then know that she will be my number one forever. Are you ready for that kind of question?"

She sucked in a breath. "Are you?" Her head started to shake no of its own accord.

"I'm not."

Her exhale of relief made him smile.

"But I might be one day. If any woman could intrigue me enough to make me wish to commit myself to only her, it would be you." He placed a hand at the side of her face. "But you would turn me down if I asked right now, and I wouldn't be able to do right by you yet."

She nodded. "We make a happy pair of friends though, don't we?"

"The best kind of friends." He smiled, and his expression was almost tender.

"Back away from her right now." Lord Lockhart's voice carried too far to too many people and had such a warning abrasive tone, Charity almost didn't recognize it. She turned.

"Act like he is being utterly ridiculous. This is very important. People are watching."

Her eyes widened.

"No, no, laugh. Laugh like he doesn't know what he is talking about."

She swallowed.

"Now."

So she laughed. And then turned to Lord Lockhart and laughed harder. "Come over here so we can laugh with you." She gestured.

Lord Wessex laughed with her.

And most everyone stopped watching them with such heightened interest.

As soon as Lord Lockhart was within whispering distance, she hissed, "What is the matter with you?"

"What are you talking about? This man was trying to exert his rakish ways."

"Keep your voice down."

"I've come to rescue you."

Lord Wessex snorted. "By making a huge fuss about nothing so that people think there's something to see and come forcing marriage on us all?"

"No, that's not what I was trying to do."

"Of course not. But that's what very nearly happened."

He looked from one to the other. "So you weren't having a romantic interlude?"

"We were having a friendship interlude." Charity didn't feel the need to tell him that it could have gone either way.

Lord Lockhart looked from one to the other. "Then you should know better." He pointed to Lord Wessex. "You particularly should know better. There needs to be space between you. You already have a reputation. Everyone is wondering when she'll give in to your charms. They're watching, thinking that your heart is about to be broken." He pointed at Charity, and she decided she very much disliked having a finger jabbing the air in her direction.

"Have I ever cared what people think? Do you think I care now? You are out of line. And don't you have your fiancée to escort home?"

"She is not my fiancée."

"So you say." Lord Wessex shook his head.

"I don't have to answer to you."

"You certainly do if you come storming out here trying to get me tied to a woman in marriage." He turned apologetic eyes to Charity. "Right after we'd just decided to be friendly to one another."

Lord Lockhart looked from one to the other. "Well, if that's the case then you're both making yourselves look ridiculous. You are a man with a known reputation. Just by association you could be ruining her."

"I really don't think it's necessary to step in here, Lord Lockhart." She tried to send warning gazes in his direction.

"But I think it is necessary. I've watched you. You're different. You're flirting for heaven's sake, Charity. And you're spending time with the biggest rake in London."

"You have no right to censure me. No right." Her fury rose up in a sudden storm that brooked no restraint. "You, with your morality, your pretend caring, when this is the most selfish act of all. You who has descended so low, how dare you come moralize with me."

His face drained of color. "Descended? There is no descension here." He stepped closer. "I need you to believe this of me."

"How can you even say such a thing?" Her voice rose.

Lord Wessex put a hand on her arm. "Might I suggest that we discuss this at a later time with fewer people in attendance?"

Charity closed her mouth, biting back a tirade of words that wished to flood the air around them, drowning out Lord Lockhart and his presumptions. "You are correct." She turned from them both. "If you'll excuse me."

Her feet hurried away, racing against the words that still fought for release. She must find Her Grace. They must leave. And she must never see that wretched Lord Lockhart again.

As the thought formed, she fought against a sob in her throat and the finality of her inclinations.

But what choice did she have? She must shut her mind and heart to Lord Lockhart forever.

CHAPTER 14

*L*ord Lockhart paced back and forth. "Descended." He sighed. "Descended." Did she believe the worst of him? His mouth pressed together. And he deserved her censure. She had a right to be angry with him. But he'd hoped to avoid her derision. Could she believe him capable of the most heinous acts? Things he'd thought he would not need to deny? Not to her. A sharp pain behind his left eye had come to reside in his head. He rubbed at his temples.

He had descended. Not in the way she might assume. But in character and quality. Charity was everything he thought well of in a woman. She was his perfect choice for a woman, smart—so very smart—witty, a conversationalist, passionate, focused on making a positive change in the world. And beautiful. She was the most beautiful person he'd ever seen. Anyone besides Charity would be a descension.

Just thinking these thoughts was bringing a pain so sharp, a longing so deep that he had to stop his pacing and clutch his chest for a moment. "Charity."

The street below his home was empty. A low-lying fog hid

the pavement from his view. He moved to the window and placed his forehead against the cool glass. Still nothing happened on the street below. Even his irrational longing that Charity would suddenly appear below in front of his house would not bring her there.

Tomorrow was the opening day of the school. Everything was in place. Volunteers were signed up. And a small contingent of Bow Street Runners and footmen were employed to keep the place safe.

Would Charity be there? Should he attend? They didn't need him. He'd done everything behind the scenes to get that place up and running. And there was no need for him to personally step foot in the place.

But he knew he would. Charity might be there. The old Charity, the woman he knew before Lord Wessex entered her life. He grimaced. It wasn't really Lord Wessex's fault that Charity had changed. The Charity before he'd broken her heart was the same woman as the Charity before she knew Lord Wessex. That's what he should refer to her as. He sighed. But should he go to the school? That was the real question here, and he didn't know the answer. She was not happy with him right now. And continuing to be in her presence when he didn't know what he offered her was not wise, or kind to either of them.

He stepped away from the silent foggy street view and climbed up into his bed.

After a sleepless night, he climbed out of bed to a chilly morning and knew he was going to the school. Whether he wanted to or not, he was going. And he wanted to. He could no sooner resist Charity or her passions or the school than his need to eat food.

And he'd done a lot to see this school got off the ground.

He wanted it to succeed almost as much as Charity did, more so if her most recent behavior was anything to go by.

He ate a quick few bites and then made his way to their new location. If all went well, they would begin that very day with their first lessons.

The minute he hopped down from his carriage, he knew something was wrong. "Wait here."

"Yes, my lord."

Children were arriving, hesitancy apparent on their faces. But the doors weren't opened.

He stepped up to a woman who was smiling at the children, reassuring them that school would start any minute, they were just waiting on a few things. When she saw him, relief crossed her expression, and Andrew hoped he would be able to assist in some way.

"We don't have the key. And we don't have the materials. And frankly, I'm not sure who is going to be doing the actual teaching."

He nodded. Who had been responsible for each of those things? If he remembered right, it was Charity. And she was nowhere to be seen. "I'm sure everything will be just fine. I would presume that the most urgent of needs would be the key."

He had signed the lease and knew the location of the owner. Perhaps the keys were still at his residence. And the books, the materials. If they did not arrive, and if there were no teachers either, then he could at the very least, teach the children, teach them something of value.

He hopped back in his carriage and gave the direction to the owner's home.

With any luck, he would catch the man at home and he

would still be in possession of the key. It would have been better if Charity had picked up the keys as planned and was on her way now to the school, but with everything that had happened between them, he couldn't be certain she would do so.

One short month ago, he would have never doubted her or anything she had committed to do.

All the way to the man's house, he felt worse about Charity, about his responsibility for her changed behavior, about how he'd behaved at the ball. He could not regret his interference with Lord Wessex. If Charity did not appreciate the precarious situation she was in with him, Andrew did.

But the larger issue bothering him should be his plans with Penny. Would he be moving forward to rescue her from herself? And therefore be subject to her flirtatious manner directed at all and sundry, as well as her obvious lack of caring for him? The more he thought about things, the more he knew he should wait, as he'd already decided. And he suspected that the longer he waited, the more he'd realize that she was not the woman for him. But a conversation was in order. He knew that. After last night especially, he knew they must converse.

Last night, he'd sent them off in his carriage. He was just not comfortable leaving Charity with Lord Wessex. While handing her up, Miss Penny had hardly spoken to him. Her mother had been all warmth and smiles. And Andrew saw more clearly the life that was opening up before him. If she couldn't be bothered to respect him or treat him with the barest civility before they were married, he had little hope for a pleasant life after. Gone was the rapport in their friendship, but that had been missing for many years.

The door opened as soon as he stopped in front of a townhome. The owner stepped outside with a package in hand. "I know you are hoping to start today. No one has come by."

"Thank you." Andrew pocketed the keys. "We hope to do much good with this location."

"I'm pleased to be a part. I never dreamed the space would be used for something so noble." He nodded. "God bless your efforts."

Andrew smiled and hopped back in the carriage. They would hurry to return and get things moving. Hopefully the children were still there, ready and waiting outside the school.

And he really hoped that the materials would have arrived.

When he returned and hopped down off the carriage, he headed toward the school at a run.

A line of children stood outside the door with a group of them running about nearby. The woman he'd left standing at the front door looked more frazzled than when he'd left her. And more children arrived from the direction of some residences he knew were nearby.

He hurried to the door, juggled his keys, finding the one that entered the front door and pushed it open.

A hoard of children rushed inside behind him. He smiled. The place was clean. "Come in here, children." He stepped through a small entryway hall and into the main space they had leased, a large area with chairs. Someone had decorated it with posters and a sign that said, "Welcome to school."

He wondered who of all the children even knew what it said. But they would soon. They would learn. And it would make all the difference.

The children stepped timidly into the room for the most part. Most of their energy and bounding about had subsided, and they walked around the space, wide eyed with curiosity. He moved up to the front. The school had no books. And as far as he could tell, no teacher.

No matter. School would go on. They had to begin. It would get better as it went along naturally, but today, they would at least lay down the rules and expectations, and if he had anything to say about it, learn something useful.

And so that is how he, Lord Lockhart, became a school-teacher.

"Class." At first, they didn't pay him any mind.

"Students." He waited. A few of them turned to him.

"Let's begin." He moved to the front of the room. "If you could each please take a seat. Choose wisely, for this will be your seat for the remainder of time in our school."

A few of them moved as quickly as possible to the very front of the room. A few others immediately chose the back. Everyone else seemed to care more about who was beside or in front or behind them. When that was at last situated, he took out a quill, inkwell and paper. "And now I will show you how to use these glorious items." He asked each of the students to say their name and he wrote it down, creating a form of chart to remember who they were and who sat in which seat. "I will need you to come every day if possible and sit in this same seat. In that way, we will learn each other's names."

He held up the quill and described its functions. "You will each get one of these."

A few of the students gasped.

"And you will learn your letters. Come every day and you will learn your basic maths. And these two things will make all the difference."

Most of them sat forward in their seats. Where had they found these children? Were they from the slums of London? Were they pickpockets like that one girl? Were they working class families? He had no way of knowing.

"And now let us begin." He stood, carrying his paper with him. "There will be times when you might feel alone." He thought of the weeks, months and years since his parents had died. "There will be times when you are suddenly asked to do things you don't know how to do. And there will be times that you might feel trapped." Like he himself felt, right in that moment. "Part of the reason this school was formed was so that you would know there will always be options. There is always a better way than to live a life of crime. Do not be trapped in the lower lives of those around you simply because they claim an association." His own words and their truth hammered through him. He intended to help them see that they could rise above their circumstances, but did his own words apply to his situation? "Help them certainly, as you can, but where assisting them brings you down into their crime-filled depths, you must rise above. You must make something of yourself. You must contribute to society in a positive way." He kept talking, kept encouraging and right in the middle of a grand example using Wellington himself, Charity stepped in the door. And with her, several servants with arms full of books and supplies, and at her side, the young pickpocket from the seedier part of London.

He grinned. She'd done it. She'd gone and found the girl. Her eyes met his, and the moment they shared was full of promise. He wasn't sure how it could be, but promise rushed between them. But promise of what? She pointed to an empty chair and the girl sat, then she moved to the front of the room. "Did I hear you telling all these children about Wellington?"

"Yes you did. Every English child needs to know about England's glorious wins."

"I'll not deny you that. No sir." She smiled and held up her copy of Shakespeare's sonnets. "And I think they could also use an introduction to the finer classics."

Between the two of them, the class consisted of an inspiring, passion-filled day of every worthy example that had inspired one or the other of them over the years. And they each had trimmed their quill and practiced making marks with it.

As their hours together came to a close and the children would be returning home for midday chores, meals, or whatever their lives held, a delicious smell filled the space and excited chatter sounded from the children. The doors opened and a line of servants entered with what looked like baskets of food. The Duchess of York herself entered their room.

Charity lifted a hand to the class. "Children, please stand." They did, eager to please.

"This is the Duchess of York; you will bow or curtsey and say, "Good morning, Your Grace.""

They did, each with a rudimentary version of some sort of attempt at respect. Andrew was proud of them. And they seemed wide-eyed with amazement to be in the presence of the duchess. He was rather shocked himself to see her there. And grateful for the footmen. It was probably time she returned to her carriage.

But she stayed and helped to pass out the food, speaking with each child.

Then Charity called a woman to the front. She wore her hair back in a bun, and seemed reasonable in every way, if not a bit cheery. "And this is Mrs. Hallford, your real teacher.

Starting tomorrow you will be trained by one of the best. Give her close attention."

Charity moved to stand beside him while they both silently watched the children talk with one another and eat their meals.

"Do I want to know how you got our young pickpocket here?"

She shook her head.

"Just as well."

"Do I want to know what you taught them for two hours before I arrived?"

He shook his head.

"Thank you." She turned to him. "Thank you for being here and getting things started. We would have lost all these children and our volunteers if you hadn't been here."

"I'm happy to see you've come, and with the supplies."

She was quiet for a moment and then sighed. "I know I've behaved in a manner which would give rise to doubt."

"Not in nearly the same manner that I have."

Pain crossed her face.

"And for that, I hope to make amends."

She turned to him. "You do?"

"I…" He was not free to say or share his doubts. "I am not as yet engaged."

She nodded. "I'm not sure what that means or if I should be pleased or not."

"Understood." From the looks of things, he may have lost her good will forever.

"I don't think you do understand."

He looked around. Most people were ignoring them, busy with eating or talking with the children, or getting to know one another. "Shall we find a place we are more free to converse?"

She followed him out of the room and into what looked like an out-of-date, unused kitchen. "This will be helpful in the school. I had forgotten about this space."

"Yes, and the food. The duchess provided?"

"She did. That woman surprises me more and more the longer I know her."

"I'm pleased to have her acquaintance. She's almost as impressive as the woman she's sponsoring."

Charity smiled. "I wish I could take hope in your complimentary words. And I don't know why I even want to."

"Ouch."

"What would you have me do? Support behavior such as yours, even when I can hardly believe it myself?"

"Behavior...just what do you think I've done?"

"I hardly dare speak the words, they are so scandalous."

He thought over his actions and what Charity might know. And he began to suspect her knowledge to be misinformed indeed. "Do you by chance think my attachment to Miss Penny to be of a stronger nature than I have expressed?"

"I know it to be so. She is with child. And I'm torn all the time between being ill that you have done that to a woman, proud that you were doing your duty by her, and sick inside that we cannot be together." Her face crumpled, and she looked away, but her eyes were dry, as though she'd resigned herself to this awful fate, had already given up on him. And why wouldn't she? He'd treated her abominably. But in some ways, he could clear up her understanding.

"Yes, she is with child. And yes, I have felt as though I'm the only person who can aid her in the way she most desires."

"I would think so." Charity almost huffed. Her disdain for him was strong indeed. And yet, so was her feeling. He had hope. Did he want hope? He studied her face. He wanted Charity. And Miss Penny certainly did not want him except for the respectability he provided. But, as he considered her actions toward him, toward Lord Wessex, toward those around them, he had begun to question whether or not she deserved the respectability his name and title provided. And would he make her child the heir? Would she then in turn raise their children? That woman? Raise his future children? He had serious doubts.

"In one thing most particularly, I would like to win back your good opinion."

She waited, her face blank, her eyes studying him.

"The child is not mine."

She gasped. And then her eyes filled with tears. She turned from him, a hand clutching her mouth, her other arm wrapped around her middle.

And he could not witness such emotion without pulling her into his arms. He turned her about to him, cradling her, holding her until she softened and received his embrace. "Not your child." Her voice murmured against his chest. Then she looked up, new tears wetting her cheeks. "Then why?"

"Do you remember the letter I showed you at the ball? The Westchesters came to me, begging for assistance, laying claim to old promises I'd made when we were children, hoping that I would rescue them." He shrugged. "And I felt I had no other choice."

She nodded. "I can see that. What choice do you have with a woman so desperate and you being in such a unique place to help her?"

"Well, I thought those same thoughts when I assumed she and I would get on together as we had, when I assumed we

were still friends and that we could create a respectable life."
He shook his head. "But I have grave concerns now. And
while I have lost the respect of the woman I love, I still do not
wish to marry a woman who I cannot respect. Nor do I think
she would be happy married to me. I have about decided to let
them know as much this evening."

Charity sucked in her breath. "This is news indeed. So you
are not engaged, nor are you planning to be?"

He shook his head.

Her chin lifted as she searched his face. "And you are not
the father of any child?"

He almost laughed but then, realizing the seriousness of
the thoughts she'd had of him, of the condemnation toward
him she must have felt, he frowned. "I would never, ever, do
such a thing. I know you have no way of knowing the other
more personal parts of my life. But I am not a man to do those
things. I will spare you knowledge of the baseness of the
actions of some in my sex. But I do not lie with women. I
have never been with any, and plan to only do such with my
wife."

Her eyes then filled with admiration, the feeling he hoped
to inspire in her forever. "And now my faith in all men has
been restored."

"All men?" He wasn't certain how pleased he wanted her
to be feeling toward any other man.

"Truly, when I thought I'd learned of the baseness of your
behavior, I then decided that all men must behave the same,
that I was naïve and idealistic to expect otherwise if you, who
I thought to be the most honorable man of my acquaintance,
had behaved so. And now that I have learned you are as good
as I suspected, my hope has been restored. To know that a
man would not only behave honorably around women but

would come to their rescue when one is in the gravest need, even despite his own desires to the contrary, I am pleased, honored even, to know you. And to think you had just given your heart to me, were about to speak to the duke, in the very throes of our love, you denied yourself to help another." Her eyes shone with such a respect, he could only drink in her admiration but at the same time, it tugged at a new guilt. For he had been about to deny Miss Penny her need, tell her mother he would no longer be moving forward with plans to marry, would be essentially sending them to a life of greater shame or significant lowering in station. And here she was, still thinking he should proceed in their rescue.

He shook his head. "I'm not sure I can continue in those noble pursuits you so ardently praise." He pulled her closer. "Not when there is such a one as you." Her eyes were full, her lips soft. He remembered so clearly the feeling of them against his own.

She moved closer. Was she open to a kiss? Could he renew their relations? Could he deny Miss Penny and at last court the woman he loved?

Her chin lifted, their lips closer, her breath but a soft puff against his mouth. She lifted her lashes, her eyes full of admiration, desire, hope. And he wanted only to answer her wishes, to fulfill her desire, to be hers forever, but in the moment he would have consumed her mouth, taken her breath in his own, her expression crumpled and she stepped away; his weight followed in a stumbled step forward.

"We cannot."

"Wha—Why not?" His hands closed around air.

"How can we leave her to such a desperate state? How could I be with you knowing in doing so I had assigned a woman to poverty? I have lived in poverty. I know."

He shook his head. "But they would not be in poverty. The father is my tenant…"

She turned from him. "I cannot. I'm sorry."

As she left the room, he could only stand in silent agony, allowing the silence around him to numb his pain. But it would never go away. He would always long for the beautiful, engaging and noble Miss Charity.

CHAPTER 15

*C*harity decided that if she could not marry Lord Lockhart, she would not get married. The other lords this Season were pleasant. They were engaging. When she thought of Lord Granville, she knew she could make a merry life with someone like him, with him. But once she'd felt the love, the desire, the respect she felt for Lord Lockhart, she knew that she could not be happy with any other. Lord Wessex had been interesting. She'd learned there was a great difference between him and Lord Lockhart. She'd been amused by him, distracted by him, but not in good ways.

She didn't need a man to continue her work at the school, didn't need a man to continue sharing truths like those she'd read in the Treatise for Women. She wouldn't have minded marrying for convenience before she'd fallen in love with Lord Lockhart, but now that she knew such a love was possible and that she'd given her heart to him, she didn't want anything other than that unity of soul.

Would she regret not having children? Certainly. But she could become the best aunt she'd ever heard of. And there was room in the castle for many a family, if not just for her in her own rooms. She suspected she would always be welcome with the Duchess of York. And, of course, with any of her sisters. Her heart pinged at the thoughts of loneliness, at knowing she would be living a life without Lord Lockhart, but she could see no other path, no other option. When she thought of the great honor of Lord Lockhart in taking on another woman, another man's child, she couldn't believe she'd ever doubted him. Certainly he would do such a thing, certainly he would be so noble.

Days later she prepared for the upcoming ball. The ball where she would tell Lord Wessex she was finished accepting any of his advances. The ball where she would continue her work, where she would talk of her causes and of the Treatise of Women, where she would begin her work for suffrage in earnest.

The ball where she would have to come to accept the presence of Lord Lockhart in her life as something other than her partner, her friend, her love. He would be someone else's and she would try to become accustomed to the idea.

She dressed with care, having come to appreciate the ability to be beautiful, to accentuate that beauty, to enjoy a lovely gown and hair designed to show off her best features. Call her vain or not, she'd come to recognize the power in beauty and she would use it for good.

When she stepped into the ballroom, and many faces turned to her, she smiled in return. Filled with confidence, she knew what good she could do for them all. She knew what she could try to encourage in all those around her. While she had their attention, she would work for good. Those thoughts filled her with joy.

Then Lord Lockhart stepped into her line of sight. And

she faltered. Perhaps her determination to live without him would be more difficult than she had planned. Nobly giving up the one you love for another was not quite as heroic as she'd imagined. His face had real longing, and she knew her expression matched, for she could not hide the love she felt for this man.

But she turned away, relieved to be distracted by a request for the first set—what used to be Lord Lockhart's set. She accepted and was led out to the floor. Their group included Lord Lockhart, Miss Penny, Lord Wessex and another vivacious debutante. Charity stood across from Lord Granville. "And what shall we be working for this evening? What manner of causes will be your purpose?" His smile was real, full, and engaging.

Miss Penny giggled at something Lord Wessex called over to her. Lord Lockhart's face was blank. But the eyes that stared into hers for just a moment shared her agony of realization. Was this to be their life now?

Partners came together and separated, Lord Granville full of his work in the House of Lords, which Charity appreciated but could feel no passion for at the moment. She would do well to encourage him. He could be one of the lords to champion a reform bill if it were ever to come to fruition.

When she stepped up to Lord Wessex, she felt nothing and indeed was annoyed at his ridiculous compliments. "I'm looking forward to our waltz." He winked. She couldn't remember promising him the waltz, but what did it matter? She'd best not dance such a set with Lord Lockhart.

At last, she stood in front of Lord Lockhart and took his hands in hers. As they moved through their steps together, she wished to dance only with him, for him, at his side forever. Her hands belonged to such a man, as did her heart and every other set. When they parted, she sighed in frustration.

The ball continued the same, with more frustration than any of the exhilarated noble feelings of sacrifice and joy she'd felt earlier.

Happily, she saw very little of Lord Wessex. She had little patience for him and his conversation at the moment.

And it seemed some in the room were talking about the school and reform all on their own. She was pleased to hear certain topics as she walked past in more than one group conversing. Perhaps good could come of all of her efforts, more than she thought possible even at the beginning of the Season.

But she found less satisfaction in it than she thought she might. She had no one to celebrate the successes with, or rather, she had lost Lord Lockhart. In the past, running to him to declare their individual victories had been half the fun.

Then Lord Wessex appeared, and the music for a waltz began. "Might I have this set, Miss Charity?" His breath smelled funny, like he might be in his cups. And as she stepped into his arms, he smelled of his usual earthy smells, but in addition, something floral tickled her nose, lavender or rose perhaps, and she wondered which specific woman had added her scent to his.

As he pulled her closer, she wasn't certain she wanted her smell to be added to his and the mystery woman's. In truth, she didn't want to be on any notch of accomplishment he might choose to boast about. She'd been lonely. He'd been friendly. But she wasn't interested in begging a conquest. Particularly not when it was so obvious he had many in mind. She tried to create more space between them, but he just laughed. "I'm not after anything nefarious. We're perfectly

JEN GEIGLE JOHNSON

presentable." He nodded with his head toward others dancing just as closely, but that meant little to her.

"Nevertheless, I am more comfortable with a little space."

"Does it have anything to do with the noble Lord Lockhart?"

Her eyes flashed with irritation. Why had Lord Lockhart caught his ire?

"No," she insisted and stepped further away.

But as they spun for a moment in the steps, he took the opportunity to pull her close again. "Charity. I find you hard to resist."

This time, no matter what she did to subtly create space, he persisted in keeping them close. Barring an arched back or a slap to his face, she was stuck.

Then as their movements continued, as the waltz progressed, she just really wanted it to end. He pulled her up against him for a moment and then let her go to a more respectable space. "We could have some fun together, indulge in our baser desires. I don't expect you to want a declaration from me, but there is nothing wrong with a hidden encounter or two. No one has to know." He searched her face, his handsome eyes growing closer to her own. Then his finger ran along her bare skin. She shrugged him off. Nothing about his attempts to win her over had any of the earlier effects. She felt only disgust and a desire to move along to the next partner as soon as possible. It was men like him who likely sent women like Miss Penny in search of an honorable rescue.

But he would take no subtle hints. Nothing she did sent him away. They danced in a darker portion of the floor, moving toward a pillar and potted plants. The seclusion might be her opportunity to make a more exaggerated escape as they were likely to garner less attention in this corner.

But he apparently viewed it as his opportunity as well. As soon as they were in the shadows, his grip tightened, and he pulled her tight up against him. With her arms pinned beneath his, she could do little to squirm away. And her only recourse now would be to shout. But such an action could very well ruin her and her opportunity to make a positive influence with any of these people again.

She sighed. "Unhand me."

"I know you want to be kissed. You've flirted right back with me. Just relax a little so we can see if we suit."

She shook her head, astounded that her earlier thoughts about kissing could be twisted in an ugly way coming from his mouth. "I already know we don't suit. Stop. Go find someone who is your equal."

But his face turned more ugly than handsome. His hand went up into her hair and gripped the back of her head.

She was at his mercy. He was going to kiss her. And she could do nothing about it.

The strongest thought, her greatest feeling of regret was that now, all the beauty of her kiss with Lord Lockhart would be erased by such a miserable human, such a horrible experience. She winced, pressed her lips together and closed her eyes.

But then Lord Wessex released her, and softer, more familiar arms cradled her.

She opened her eyes. "Wilfred."

"Charity." His intense eyes were full of love, caring, concern. "Are you well?"

She nodded. "Now I am. Oh, thank you." She looked around. Lord Wessex turned a corner, rubbing his face. "Did you hit him?"

"Just enough. He'll be fine."

"I'm not worried one ounce for that miserable version of a human. He was going to force himself." She choked, her words caught in her throat, and she realized she was much more affected than she had thought.

But he pulled her closer. "I'm sorry. I should have been here sooner."

She shook her head against him. "Not your fault. Where have you been? I never know where you go at these balls."

"I was ending all relations with Miss Penny."

She jerked her gaze up to him. "You were?" Dare she hope? Did that make her a bad person? Oh, she wanted him, more than life itself.

"Yes, you see, if he'd kissed you, yours would not be the first lips he'd tasted this evening."

She gasped as the realization of what he meant sunk in. "Miss Penny?"

"Yes, and a most passionate example of what those two are capable of together."

"Together? Do you think they will make a go of it?"

"They will."

She studied him. "How can you be sure?"

"I've exerted some influence over his debtors, and after seeing his and Penny's shameless attempts to be together in front of all and sundry, decided they are made for one another."

She shook her head. "And her pains from the other evening?"

"She seems to be well and truly cured of them."

"So, they'll marry?"

"I believe so."

"You're free?" She could hardly keep her voice down. And she no longer cared who saw or who knew. The man she

170

loved was free from previous entanglements. He was free to pursue her.

"I'm not free." He shook his head.

The hope in her heart clouded. "No?"

"I have not been free since the moment I met you, not free to love anyone...but you."

Her smile grew, and relief filled her heart. "Oh no?"

"No. I'm yours, Charity. Please, be my wife."

She gasped a half laugh, half shock, sort of noise. And then she realized they were attracting attention. And she was pleased as could be about it.

"Do you know that people are watching?" She focused only on him.

"I don't even care."

She laughed. "Nor do I." She stepped closer. "I love you, Wilfred."

"I love you too, Charity. Now put me out of my misery. Will you marry me? Am I enough? Can I make you happy?"

"Yes, in every way yes. I can be only yours. Yours or alone. Yes, I will marry you."

He studied her face for but a moment more and then their lips came together without another thought. Charity thought her feet might float away, taking them to the clouds. People around them began to clap, and she dipped her head in embarrassment, her smile growing.

Then the Duke of York's voice carried out over them all. "What is this?"

Lord Lockhart turned, taking her hand in his. "This is me, asking if I might have a word with you in private, in regards to my love for Miss Charity."

His Grace did not look as amused as others around them

seemed to be, but he nodded. "About time." And then he turned his back on them both.

Charity breathed out in relief, squeezing his hand, and hugging his arm close. "Can this really be happening?"

"I hope so. I cannot live another minute thinking anything else."

"Nor I." She hugged his arm closer.

They accepted many rounds of congratulations from others in the room, including Lord Granville. He clapped Lord Lockhart on the back. "I look forward to all the good we can do."

"I as well, thank you, Granville."

Until the whole evening felt a bit like an engagement announcement party. And Charity knew she couldn't be happier. As the evening was about to end, and their carriages had been called, Lord Lockhart leaned closer. "There is something I have to tell you."

"Oh no. Should I be concerned?"

"Not at all, it is simply to explain that no one calls we Wilfred. Except you."

Her eyes widened. "How can that be?"

"It just is. While I love hearing it from your lips, really, my name is Andrew."

Charity tipped back her head and laughed. "I've never been so entertained." But then she stopped and stepped closer. "But I've fallen in love with you, thinking you are Wilfred. Perhaps the name has stuck."

He lifted her hand to his lips. "Then I shall be Wilfred."

EPILOGUE

*G*race Standish should have been happy about Charity's wedding. She should have been rejoicing with the others. But in truth, she had grown tired of all of it, the marriages, the seeking for marriage, the Seasons. With the time finally upon her to have a Season herself, she wanted nothing to do with it.

But Lord Lockhart and Charity were two of the happiest people she'd ever seen. They were perhaps the most suited of all the couples in her family. He not only understood her intelligence and her need to study every sort of topic and discuss it and all its intricacies for hours on end, he reveled in it. She'd never seen a man more proud than he was when she bested every man in the room with her knowledge of a particular battle in which Wellington had done some remarkable thing. Grace laughed. She was happy for her sister.

June came to stand beside Grace, her arm going around her shoulder. "And now you're next."

Grace didn't know what to say. Except that she didn't want to be courted. She didn't want to be a part of a Season.

That was just asking to get hurt in one way or another. She was just asking to be ruined, forced, or kidnapped. No one talked about it much, but she would never forget how easily she'd been fooled by Lord Kenworthy, how quickly he'd whisked her away and how closely she'd come to being miserable forever.

"Maybe you can choose him for me." Her eyes widened in hope. She knew what June would say. That none of the sisters needed a marriage of convenience, they'd all at last had the opportunity and the means to marry for love, even Lucy, who'd chosen to marry their stable hand. But instead of all the typical reassurances she had heard June say before to all their other sisters, she squeezed Grace. "We can if you would like."

And those words, that simple response had filled Grace with relief. She nodded. "Thank you."

Charity and Lord Lockhart came running over, Charity's dress flowing all around her, a white beauty like few had ever seen, Lord Lockhart looking about ready to burst with happiness. "I love you, little Grace." Charity kissed her cheek. "June."

"So happy for you!" Grace waved a hand as the two ran off to climb in their carriage ready to be happy for the rest of their lives.

Grace's cheeks hurt from smiling. "We are blessed indeed."

"Yes we are." June wiped the tears from her cheeks.

Charity was going to live in London. Neither had much desire to return to the Lockhart estate. They were making plans to build their own new estate, but they hadn't decided on the perfect location. Grace hoped it would end up in Brighton. But they had no need. If they came to Brighton, everyone could stay at the castle.

No matter what, Grace knew they would be happy, and that's all that mattered, as long as she still got to see her sisters.

Charity blew kisses to everyone cheering them on for their departure in their new life together. And Lord Lockhart threw the contents of a bag of coins high into the air.

Everyone cheered even louder. Lucy and Kate joined Grace and June so that four Standish sisters stood in a line to wave farewell. Morley, Gerald and Amelia, Logan, and Conor stood nearby. Grace couldn't help but feel that all she needed, all she would ever need was right there in her life.

"Goodbye!" She waved. The others cheered along with her.

And Lord and Lady Lockhart rode off into a real-life sunset.

CHAPTER 1 THE EARL'S WINNING WAGER

*M*orley stared at his best friend, waiting for the man to look up from his cards. Gerald was losing terribly. And Morley wasn't sure if he should feel guilty or victorious. His friend had just thrown most of a new inheritance from his distant cousin on the table, almost as if he wished to give it away.

Despite Gerald being the Duke of Granbury with significant holdings to his name, Morley wasn't comfortable taking so much—even in something as unbiased as a card game. But his friend smiled so large it looked like his cheeks hurt. Morley's hurt just looking at him.

"How can you smile when you're losing abominably?" Lord Morley frowned at him.

"I have leave to be happy so soon after my own wedding."

"But you don't have leave to gamble away your living, even to your best friend."

"I'm hardly close to losing a living."

Lord Morley raised his eyebrows. The other lords at the table stared greedily at the back of Gerald's cards. But even though Lord Morley shook his head, none too subtly, Gerald pushed all the remaining chips and his slips of paper into the center.

"Included in this are some holdings in the south."

Lord Morley narrowed his eyes.

Gerald fanned out his cards. "Good, but"—he smiled even broader—"not good enough." Then each of the men laid out their cards. Gerald beat Lord Oxley soundly, as Morley suspected he knew he would. Then Lords Harrington and Parmenter threw their cards down. That left Morley's cards. Morley had won. Gerald knew he'd won. He eyed him above his cards. "What is this about?"

"Lay out your cards, man. On with it." Gerald's smile couldn't grow any larger, and even though Morley had just grown significantly more wealthy, he didn't trust his oldest friend.

Morley fanned out his cards and narrowed his eyes. "What are you doing?"

Gerald tipped his glass back and drained its contents. "Losing to my best friend. Come now. It's time for us to return home. Her Grace wants me home early."

"How is she feeling?"

Gerald's face clouded, and Morley regretted the question. Since the man had lost his first wife during childbirth, the prospect of doing it all over again loomed in his mind at all hours. Morley talked to him of it often enough. "She seems in the very prime of health. No one has looked healthier."

"No need to speak optimism in my ear. I know she is well, but then, so was Camilla. All we can do is wait and see. Amelia so wanted a child, and I love my wife too much to leave her alone. So there we have it."

Morley clapped him on the back as they stepped out of

White's. "Do you ever consider it odd that when youth, we used each other's titles in preparation for the moment the great weight would fall on our shoulders? And now. You still call me Morley, but I … don't call you anything but Gerald." He laughed trying to lighten the mood.

"You will always be Morley. Even your mother calls you Morley." He laughed. "Why is that?"

"I couldn't guess. Maybe she loves the title?" He shrugged. "Now, enough mystery. Tell me, what did I just win? What's this all about? These holdings in the south?"

"Remember our visit to Sussex?"

Morley half nodded, and then he stopped dead in the street. "When we went to save you from Lady Rochester? And we paid a visit to a family of ladies?" His eyes narrowed. Unbidden, Miss Standish's face came into his mind. "What did you do?"

"I inherited their castle, if you recall."

"I recall a heap of rubble with a few standing rooms."

"Well, we've been fixing it up, and the ladies are just about ready to move in. Five women, all of age. June, the eldest, is not quite twenty three, the youngest sixteen. You won the whole lot of them, with some other holdings besides. The winnings should cover the remaining repairs and upkeep for a time as well."

"I won't take it."

"You have no choice. There were witnesses."

Morley was silent for so long he hoped Gerald began to half suspect he'd truly overstepped his generosity at long last. Then he shook his head. "I know what you're doing, and she doesn't want anything to do with me."

"I don't know what you're talking about."

"And she will want even *less* to do with me if she thinks

she is in any way beholden to me, so whatever plans you have going, you can just take back your properties and your pesky family of women and leave me in peace."

"Morley, you're my oldest and best friend. Would I really foist these women on you if I didn't think it would make you the happiest of men? They're from the Northumberland line. Excellent family heritage. The Queen herself takes an interest in their well-being."

"I care not for any of such nonsense, and you know it. You are not to be a matchmaker. It doesn't suit you. And you're terrible at it."

"How would you know, since I've never attempted such a roll until now?"

"So you admit it?"

"I admit nothing. Now, come, don't be cross. You'll upset Amelia."

"Oh, that is low, bringing your wife's condition into this."

They stepped into the townhome, where Simmons took their hats and gloves and overcoats. Gerald waved Morley in. "Thank you for staying with us while you're in town."

"At times, I prefer your home to my own situation."

"You're a good son, though."

Morley hoped he was, though his mother was tiring at best and liked to have her fingers in most aspects of his dealings. He loved her, and felt she was happy in her life, such as it was.

A soft, melodic voice called, "Gerald? Is that you?"

Amelia stepped out into the foyer. "And Morley." She clapped her hands, and the smile that lit her face filled the room.

He accepted her kiss on the cheek and watched as Gerald turned all of his focus to his wife.

Morley bowed. "I will bid you good night. Tomorrow, Gerald, we will discuss your sneaking ways."

"What has he done?" Amelia could only look with love at the Duke, and Morley felt, for a moment, a pang of loneliness.

"I've done nothing. Morley is just a sore winner."

Morley refused to say more. He bowed to Amelia and made his way up the stairs. Before he reached the first landing, he turned. "Oh, and Gerald?"

Gerald turned from his wife for a brief moment.

"When are we to go visit my winnings?"

"Oh, you're on your own with that one, Morley. They will much prefer you to me at any rate." He turned back to Her Grace, and Morley continued up the stairs, his mood darkening with every step.

Gerald had gone too far—in some mad effort to match him with a woman who really had no more interest in Morley than she did dancing a quadrille. June Standish was as practical as he'd seen a person.

He sighed.

And far handsomer than any he'd yet laid eyes on. Her hair was gold—it looked to be spun from the metal itself—and her eyes large, doe-like. He had lost all sense of conversation when he first saw her. It had taken many minutes for him to gain his faculties enough to speak coherently, but she had seemed entirely unaffected. And so that was it for them.

He could only imagine her reaction when he returned to let her know a new gentleman, he himself, was now lord over her life and well-being. Gerald should not toy with others' lives. He needed to be stopped. But Morley wasn't going to be the one to stop him. They'd carried on in their friendship in just this way since they'd known each other. Perhaps he could appeal to Amelia. She had more control over the man than anyone.

What did he need with a decrepit, dilapidated castle? It was an old seat of the royal dukes, so there was a certain level of prestige associated with the place—and with the women. They were of the ancient Normandy family lines. Someone somewhere in their family had wasted their money and left nothing for the line to live off of, but it was still considered an elevated situation if you were on friendly terms with any of the Sisters of Sussex, as they were called.

Sleep did not come easily, and morning was not friendly to Morley's tired eyes and mind. Instead of breaking his fast with Gerald and Amelia, he left for a walk. Oddly, his steps took him to Amelia's old tearoom. They let it out, once she was to become the duchess, and someone else ran the establishment instead. As he stood in the doorway, he almost walked away without entering. What was he doing in a tearoom? Colorful dresses filled the shop to bursting.

"Lord Morley!" With the swish of skirts, a woman's hands were on his arm. "What a pleasant surprise. You must join us for tea. We are discussing the upcoming McAllister ball."

He allowed himself to be led to their table, and when four expectant female eyes turned their hopeful expression toward him, he could only smile and say, "How perfect, for I was just wondering about the details."

"Then you are attending?" Lady Annabelle's eyes lit with such a calculating energy, he shifted in his seat, eyeing the door for a second.

"I am, indeed."

"How provident. Then we shall all be there together. You remember we all became acquainted at the opera one week past. Miss Talbot, Miss Melanie—"

"And Lady Annabelle. Naturally, we are acquainted. It is a pleasure to see you again. I hope your mother is well?"

Lady Annabelle poured his tea, and his mind could not leave the family he'd just won charge of. What sort of women was this new family of sisters? He'd been most impressed with them when considering them as Gerald's wards, of a sort. But now that he owned the house they lived in, he felt a whole new interest in their deportment. Could they pour a man's tea? Stand up well with the other ladies at a ball? Would he be able to marry them off? That was the crux of it. And dash it all, why must he be concerned with the marrying off of anyone? He was in over his head. He needed help. He could appeal to Amelia's sense of grace, but she would have little knowledge of the ways of the *ton*.

The women chattered around him, and he almost sloshed his tea in the saucer when he heard mention of the very women who so aggravated his thoughts.

"They call them the Sisters of Sussex."

"Really? Who are they?"

"The Duke of Northumberland's relations, from a royal line. They are the talk of the *ton* and favorites of many of the noble families. We ourselves have stopped by with some of last season's gowns."

"Five sisters, you say? And they live in the old castle?"

"A cottage nearby. The castle is being renovated, though. I heard the Duke of Granbury has become involved." Lady Annabelle turned to him. "Do you know much about the sisters?"

He cleared his throat and shifted in his seat. "I have met them."

The other ladies leaned forward, eyes on him.

"And I found them charming," he said. "I think you know

more about their history than I. Though I do know the castle will be repaired and livable, as it deserves to be. It's a remarkable structure."

Miss Talbot fanned her face. "I should like to visit. I love old buildings and their architecture."

"Do you?" Morley tipped his head to her. She was a pretty sort of woman. Chestnut curls lined her face, and deep brown eyes smiled at him.

"Yes, I like to draw them, and then study them after."

"Interesting. Perhaps we shall meet up there sometime."

"Oh?" Lady Annabelle rested a hand on his arm. "Will you be spending much time in Brighton?"

He hadn't planned on it yet. He'd hoped to stay as far away as possible until his mind wrapped around this new responsibility. But he changed his plans in the moment. "I think I shall." He looked into each of their faces. They were pleasant women. They seemed kind—unassuming, perhaps. "Might I ask for some assistance?"

"Certainly." Lady Annabelle's eyes gleamed.

"I wonder, if I were to assist the ladies—any ladies—to be prepared for a smallish Season in Brighton, do they have a dressmaker or shops enough down there?"

"Oh, certainly. Not nearly as grand or varied as London, but a woman can make do with what Brighton has to offer. The Brighton Royal Pavilion has brought much of the *ton* and a higher level of prestige to the area."

"Thank you."

Their gossip-loving ears seemed to perk right up and all three pairs of eyes looked on him a bit too keenly. He resisted adjusting his cravat. "So, who will be attending the McAllister ball? And have each of you found partners already for your dances?"

The chatter grew more excited, and they listed all the people who were coming or might be coming, depending on the attendance of others. He lingered as long as was polite, and then excused himself from this cheery group.

He would go check in on his mother, though he planned not to mention his new winnings at the table, and then make arrangements to travel down to visit the Standish sisters. God willing, he could establish good solutions for their situation and living and have them well in hand within a few weeks.

CHAPTER 2 THE EARL'S WINNING WAGER

*M*iss June Standish ran her finger down the ledger, calculating expenses, the infernal drafts in the cottage sending a trail of gooseflesh up her arms. She pulled her thickest shawl tighter around her shoulders. The hour was early yet. None of her sisters had ventured downstairs, but their remaining in bed might have more to do with the chill in the air than them being asleep. Though she assumed her youngest sister, Grace, continued to sleep soundly.

They could probably burn more wood. They had a budget for it. Ever since the Duke of Granbury inherited their cottage and castle, things had improved. But they didn't have enough servants to get the fire going in the morning. And the way she looked at it, once you left your bed, you may as well venture downstairs to be in the kitchen where it was warmest anyway. Perhaps they should hire another servant.

The castle renovations were under way. She wasn't certain she wanted to move with her sisters into another infernally drafty place, but His Grace had assured her the living areas of the castle would be superior to her current situation. They were scheduled to move in next month.

He had also assured her that her chances of marrying would improve if they lived in the castle. Anyone who didn't know their royal connections would be made aware, simply by their inhabiting the old seat.

She sighed. If only she could see each of her sisters happily married.

Grace stepped into the kitchen, her blankets wrapped around her.

June stood. "Grace, what are you doing up so early?"

"I couldn't sleep. This house makes noises."

"We've been here long enough for you to know the noises don't mean a thing."

"They have to mean something. I was more worried about them when we first arrived, but I'll admit, sometimes I see an old, weathered sailor with absurdly long fingernails scratching on my window."

"Goodness. You do have an imagination."

Grace shrugged and sat as close to June as she could. "What are you working on?"

"I'm determining if we need another servant."

"A lady's maid?"

June laughed. "And what do we need one of those for?"

"To do our hair, help us dress…"

"We have each other."

"But a maid could do the modern styles, help us look our very best. His Grace said we'd be having a Season."

"The others will. You are still too young to be out."

She groaned in frustration. "Really, am I too young for everything?"

"No, you are just the right age to help me get some water boiling."

"A cook. We should hire another assistant for cook."

June had thought of it. "I think the castle has its own staff as well, so when we blend there, we can work out different responsibilities among the staff. It's just one more month."

Grace grinned. "I can't wait. I love the castle. And then no one can forbid me to enter or explore, because we will all live there."

"That is true. There will be areas blocked off for safety reasons while the renovations continue, but we shall have a rather large area that is our own living space."

"Do you think this is what Uncle wanted for us?"

"Perhaps." June toyed with her quill. They had all loved their uncle, the Earl of Beaufort, as old and confused as he sometimes became. He had swept in and picked up the pieces of their broken lives, hugged the loneliness out of them, and helped them feel centered and loved. His loss was one of their greatest, almost to the intensity of losing their parents. "Regardless of his intent, we are making the best of it, are we not?"

"Yes. I'm just grateful we have each other." She curled closer and rested her head on June's shoulder.

"I feel the same, sweet." She tipped her head so it rested on the top of Grace's. They sat thus for a moment more. Then June knew it was time to begin the day. "We have our studies this morning. And our dancing instruction this afternoon."

"Will we ever have a man to practice with?"

"Someday, when we dance the real thing." June laughed. "Am I not a good enough dance partner?"

"You're excellent." Grace's tone and expression said just the opposite.

"I hope one day to see you all happily wed. You know that. Perhaps with the duke's help, we can secure good matches for each one of you."

"And you." Grace's large and caring eyes made June's heart clench.

"You are a dear, but I might feel happiest just to see each one of you settled."

"And perhaps one of us will marry gobs of money, enough to care for us until our dying days."

"That would be wonderful, but the only thing I ask is you also marry for happiness."

Grace nodded. "But don't you think all manner of happiness could be found, if the living is comfortable?"

"I suppose." June didn't wish to fill her sister's head with romantic fancies. For a woman in the Standish sisters' financial state could not afford to be romantic in her choice of marriage partner. But they could insist on happiness, on comfort or security. She hoped they could at least strive for that.

After a modest breakfast, all five sisters met in the music and school room. June smiled at them all. Every now and then, she had to relax about their many worries and just appreciate the good that surrounded them. Grace, Lucy, Kate, and Charity were the best of women, the very best she knew, at any rate, and she was intensely proud of every one.

They'd converted an additional sitting room to their place of projects. On one end, the easels were set, with large, billowing fabric covering the floor to catch the paint. They had a pianoforte, a smaller harp, needlepoint, and on the other end of the room, a large blackboard and a bookshelf full of books. Their library might be small compared to some, but it was full of June's most prized possessions.

As the only Standish daughter who'd had a governess, and she for only a short amount of time, June spent an hour every day working on their deportment, the rules of society, their manners, and their general instruction in the ways of a gently bred lady.

"And what if I do not wish for a gently bred man?" Charity's stubborn streak grew the longer they lived in Sussex. June wasn't sure what drove her stronger sensibilities.

"I just want you happy, and in most cases, that means with enough food on the table, an established place to live, and a good man. If that can be found in the working classes, then all the happier I will be, since you profess to prefer such a life."

"'Such a life.' What a snob you are, June."

"Tsk. She's not a snob." Kate shifted her skirts. "She does well by us to show us how to present ourselves. I, for one, do not wish to be embarrassed when next the Duchess of York stops in."

"Oh, she is the utmost. That woman's nose is so far in the air, I'm surprised she can walk." Charity shook her head.

"We are grateful for their goodness to us. All our fine dresses come from her and the others."

"Yes." Kate slumped in her seat. "Last year's fashions."

"And still plenty ostentatious." Charity lifted her skirts. "Who needs embroidery on the hem? Lace I can see, but embroidery? It just gets dirty on these roads and is impossible to wash out."

"Then don't be wearing the embroidery while out exploring the dirty roads." Kate poked her needle into the handkerchief she was sewing.

"What are you making?" June leaned closer.

"I'm hoping to have a stack of these for when we go to dinners and balls in Brighton. Then a man could know where to return it." She'd sewn pretty flowers on the edges, as well as her initials and Northumber Castle.

"That's lovely." June lifted her book. "Now, allow me to finish." She read to them from Shakespeare, and had more interest than in her previous descriptions of the early royal lineage. They would follow up the literature lesson with French, and then lunch.

In a break in her reading, Grace piped up, "We'll have dancing this afternoon."

"Do we have Jacques to come instruct us?" Charity's hopeful expression gave June pause.

"No, not today. We will be working on the country dances. And those are simple enough to memorize without Jacques. He will come next week for the waltz."

"Oh, I love the waltz." Grace clapped her hands together.

"As do I." Kate put down her embroidery, her black, shiny curls bouncing at her neck. "Do you think we could have a new bonnet for the promenade on Tuesday?"

"What promenade?" June searched her memory for mention of a promenade.

"Oh, come, June. Pay attention. Prinny will be back in town, and everyone will begin walking up and down the green. Everyone who is here will attend. It is the prime location for us to be seen and make an impression." She paused in a rather dramatic manner. "*If* we make a good impression."

"I wish to make a good impression. Do you think we need new bonnets?" Grace looked from June to Kate and back.

"I think we will make the best impression, no matter what kind of bonnets are on our heads." June set the book aside. But inside she worried about just such a thing. Would they be able to be seen as anything other than charity to the gentry?

Perhaps a bonnet would help? She shook her head. Everything seemed so overwhelming at times. She'd never had a Season herself. Her parents had fallen ill, and were taken from them around the time she would have started to prepare. What did she really know about any such thing? "No matter what, we must be a Standish daughter, women with a heritage to be proud of."

Stenson stepped into their small parlor. "The Duchess of Sussex here to see you."

June sucked in her breath. The arrival of the Duchess was a mixed blessing. "You know how we must receive her."

They all stood taller, painted blank expressions on their faces, and moved to the front sitting room, reserved almost solely for visits from the nobility—and in this case, the royal family. As soon as they were situated, each with a different manner of amusement—embroidery, reading, drawing, and two opposite a chess board, though no one had moved a single piece in ages—Stenson opened their door. "The Duchess of Sussex."

The Standish sisters stood and curtsied.

Their guest smiled, and her eyes twinkled. "Oh, my lovelies, my dears. Let me have a look at you." She held out her hands. She kept such a youth and vigor about her, June had vowed to do the same. Kate admired her clothing. Lucy coveted her title, and Charity looked at her with great suspicion.

June curtseyed again. "It is good to see you, Your Grace. You do us honor by your visit."

"I find so much happiness aiding in your situation, such as it is." She studied them for a moment, and June wondered if she'd break out in tears right then. "Oh, and aren't you the most deserving." She placed hands on her heart. "To think, so reduced in situation, so noble in bearing. You are all to be commended for your fortitude."

"Thank you, Your Grace." June dipped her head. "Would you care for some tea? Coffee?"

"Oh, thank you, if you can spare some."

"We have ample." June nodded to their maid, who waited just outside the door.

As soon as Her Grace was seated, she adjusted her skirts. They flowed in an elegant manner to the floor. The delicate flowers that lined her hemline, the tiny sparkles of gems which glittered when the sun touched them, must have been fascinating to June's most fashion-conscious sister, Kate.

"Has the Duchess of York been by?" The Duchess of Sussex asked, as though she didn't care, but June knew their answer would pester and bother her for days.

And Charity did too. "She has, and she brought us the most exquisite gowns. They must have been her own, they were so lovely. To everyone who asks, we must positively gush about the Duchess of York and her deep generosity."

"Oh, did she? That's nice, isn't it? Hmm." She narrowed her eyes and waved her hand. A servant in the Sussex livery appeared in the doorway as if summoned from invisibility. "Please bring in the packages."

He nodded.

"Well, I have brought some of my own."

Kate gasped and placed hands at the side of her face. "Oh, thank you, Your Grace, for your sense of style is exquisite. I have been studying just now how perfectly you wear your clothing. Of all the ladies, you are my most favorite."

The duchess beamed. "I appreciate a woman who understands the finer details of fashion. Which one are you?" She lifted a quizzing glass. "Come here."

Kate almost tripped over herself to rush to Her Grace's side.

"Ah, yes. Miss Kate, is it?"

"Yes, Your Grace. If it pleases you."

"You shall have my brooch."

Their sister Lucy gasped, but June waved her to hush.

"Thank you." Kate's curtsy was low and grateful.

"I have brought dishes as well, and some food from cook's kitchen. We live near enough you should be recipients of our finest."

"Thank you. You could not dote upon more grateful servants."

"Now that we are here in Brighton for a smaller Season, I plan to visit often. Whenever we are in our Sussex estate, we will be sure to pay you a call."

"We will look forward to the honor."

The tea service arrived. "How would you like your tea?"

They ate and sipped, and the duchess filled them in on the gossip of the *ton* and from London.

"Oh, you sisters would love London. Imagine a Season in Town. Wouldn't that be so exciting! I cannot fathom how your forbearers could leave you with so little, so paltry your opportunities to attend such delights as a Season. I know a handsome earl. He would be perfect for one of you." She clucked. "A pity you could not go even one Season."

"Yes, pity." Charity's look of mock sorrow almost made June laugh, and she hoped the duchess would not see the duplicitous expression. Did the duchess not know the hurt her words could cause? Or did she really think the sisters didn't feel their situation keenly enough without her comments?

They chatted a few moments more and then bade the woman goodbye. She left piles of things in the entry. June should be grateful for the gifts, and she was. But unless the gowns fit, it was an expense to alter them, or a lot of work for the sisters. Kate was becoming quite proficient with a needle.

After lunch, and once the duchess departed, the sisters gathered back in the music room. Grace sat at the piano. "But I wish to dance this time. Someone give me a chance to practice the steps."

"We will, but after the rest of us have a go. You're the youngest."

"I know." Grace frowned. "So you all keep saying."

"Well, there is less a need for you to learn, as you won't even be dancing."

"Thank you, Lucy."

"We all know Lucy is going to marry money, and then the rest of us won't have to worry about getting married." Charity waved her hand in Lucy's direction.

"I'd like to get married." Kate pouted. "And so would everyone else, I imagine, including June."

"Yes, even me. But we'll worry about the rest of you first." She hid her sadness. *Even June.* She was not a spinster, not even close to being on the shelf, but she just didn't think she could spend the effort getting herself married when she had so many others to be concerned with.

Grace started in on a well-known country dance, and June called out the steps while she did them. "You see? I start, and then I must add my own flair here. You watch and repeat."

The girls stepped together with imaginary partners, waited while their partners would have done the same, and then repeated. It was a bit confusing at times, but it worked well enough.

Then Stenson, their very young butler, stepped into the room. "A Lord Morley to see you."

The girls froze. Kate whispered, "Who?"

June's heart skipped, and the pause between beats thundered in her chest. "I—" Her voice cracked. "I do believe that is Morley?"

"The nice man who came with the duke? He's an earl?"

"Yes, he was introduced as such, but His Grace called him Morley so often, the 'earl' part didn't stick. I do hope we did not follow suit and omit his title." Lucy clucked. "To neglect to use a man's title without permission is an insult in the highest order."

"Yes, thank you, Lucy." June stood and straightened her dress, urging the girls to rise as well. They rolled the carpet back where it should be and patted down their hair. "Send him in, Stenson."

He nodded. "Very good, miss."

"Does anyone else think Stenson looks like a young boy playing a part?" Charity giggled.

"Hush." June shook her head.

And in walked Lord Morley, the man she'd thought of constantly since their meeting, the most handsome man of her albeit limited acquaintance. He filled the room with his large stature, his strong shoulders, his brilliant jawline, with the crisp white of his cravat brushing against it. His gaze flitted through the sisters and rested on June. And then the corner of his mouth lifted in a soft smile. "Miss Standish." He bowed. "Miss Charity, Miss Lucy, Miss Kate, and Miss Grace."

Grace giggled from behind the piano.

They all curtsied.

Then June stepped forward. "We are so happy you have come. Please, take a seat. Would you like some tea?"

"Tea would be wonderful, thank you."

Grace tripped off to the kitchen to inform their cook.

And June wasn't sure she could form words. Why had he come? The idea he would arrive to pay a social call filled her with hope, a hope she tried to tamp out.

"Tell us the news of London." Kate asked all their visitors to talk of London. Usually she was most seeking news of fashion, but as Lord Morley would likely know little of those kinds of details, June supposed Kate would be satisfied with whatever snippets she could glean.

"Things are warming up in London, just enough to almost be pleasant." He laughed. "Not many families stayed on. I expect the Season to pick up in high form in a month or two. I hear many of the families have come to Brighton."

"We hear the same." Kate fluffed her skirts. "In fact, we were just talking of doing a promenade on the green tomorrow. Will you be staying long?"

"I will be here for a few weeks or more, I believe." His gaze flitted to June's.

June didn't respond, for she wasn't sure what to say at all to his statement. She was most desperately pleased, but so impatient with herself for thinking in such a way. Charity kicked her ankle. June started. "I'm happy to hear it. Would you care to join us tomorrow in our promenade? Like Miss Kate said, you are likely to see most everyone from Brighton at one point or another on the green."

"I should very much enjoy the outing, thank you."

The tea arrived, and June busied herself with the pouring. Why had he come? She couldn't account for it. And even though his gaze rested on her more than anywhere else, nothing could make sense in her mind as to why that would be.

. . .

READ the rest here The Earl's Winning Wager

FOLLOW JEN

Jen's other published books

The Nobleman's Daughter
Two lovers in disguise

Scarlet
The Pimpernel retold

A Lady's Maid
Can she love again?

His Lady in Hiding
Hiding out at his maid.

Spun of Gold
Rumpelstilskin Retold

Dating the Duke
Time Travel: Regency man in NYC

Charmed by His Lordship
The antics of a fake friendship

Tabitha's Folly
Four over-protective brothers

To read Damen's Secret
The Villain's Romance

Follow her Newsletter

Follow Jen's Newsletter for a free book and to stay up to date on her releases. https://www.subscribepage.com/y8p6z9

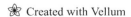

Made in the USA
Las Vegas, NV
07 March 2022